THE IMMANENT WORLD

a compendium of the weird, the horrific and the bizarre

AOE STUDIOS

The Immanent World

Cover design by Mary Jacobowitz:

Facebook.com/mary.jacobowitz

AOE Studios

9200 Owings Park Drive

Suite K

Owings Mills, MD 21117

ISBN 13: 978-0-9829533-1-0

Printed in the United States of America

First Edition: 2012

contents

immanence not imminent

The title of this book caused confusion from the first it was put to paper. *The Immanent World*—when I told my friends the title of the book they immediately thought "imminent, something is coming". However, this is not the focus of this collection of fiction and art.

Immanence is a transcendental concept, often having to do with the inherent divinity of mankind. Instead of looking outward to the "other world", it suggests that these things dwell within.

Another theme of immanence is that the world within often does not affect the world outside. Personally, I find this a theme that is lacking in modern entertainment. All too often, western pop culture seems to intertwine the two to the extent that it's often hard to separate fiction from reality. Some even believe there isn't a divide between the two and that fiction should be reality.

The notion of immanence however allows us to explore the themes of darkness and light, passion and love, fear and horror without causing us to duplicate the experience in real life. Delving into these fictional worlds can bring enlightenment or entertainment, but as the notion of immanence suggests, they do not determine our day-to-day actions and thoughts.

This is not to say that the imagination should be locked inside the mind. Quite the contrary, the imagination should influence thought without a doubt. But there is a difference to influencing thought and emulating actions. In fact, you can argue that a step-by-step emulation of what we experience from journeying into the dreams and illusions of talented artists can lead to a *lessening* of imagination.

Speaking as a character speaks, reciting lines from a film, taking on the ideology of a poet or a musician because they craft their work expertly is simply copying someone else's thoughts, not an expansion of your own imagination.

At its best, immanence can teach us to learn from the wonders of art and expand the transcendent and metaphysical worlds within our own minds, allowing them to burst forth in vibrant colors never known before.

As for the work here, it is a collection that was chosen based on artists and writers that struck me as talented and *off-center*. As the subtitle suggests, this is a collection weird works, twisted dreams and new takes on old ideas.

The four short stories are quite different in tone. Some are dripping with drama, others delve into metaphysical mysteries, and some are bubbling with violence. All four stories put a new twist on something that's familiar. Initially, a reader can feel they've walked these roads before, but soon you realize you're on a side street that has no road sign.

The same can be said for the poetry presented here by three fine young writers. The dreams of today's youth are quite different than even a generation prior, and this can be seen clearly in the emotional, philosophical and (sometimes) humorous writings in this collection.

Visually, the artists who have contributed to *The Immanent World* come from slightly different disciplines. Some of the art is meant to disturb, some is meant to simply entertain. There is a high level of detail in all the digital artwork presented here and those details can be overlooked if passed by quickly. I encourage the reader to take their time with the imagery.

The Immanent World has proven to be an instructive project and truly enjoyable to put together. This is a coffee table book for those who aren't shy about delving into the dark and light places within themselves.

– KC Hunter

December 2011

The prior commentary is that of this particular author and does not necessarily reflect the views of other contributors.

kevin hopson

Prior to hitting the fiction scene in 2009, Kevin was a freelance writer for several years, covering everything from finance to sports. His debut work, **World of Ash**, was released by MuseItUp Publishing in the fall of 2010. Since then, he has had two other short stories released by the same publisher - **Earthly Forces** and **Early Release for Bad Behavior**. Kevin's contributing anthology story, *A Gut Feeling*, is actually a follow up to Early Release for Bad Behavior. He focuses primarily on the science fiction, dark fiction, horror, paranormal, and crime fiction genres.

http://museituppublishing.com/musepub

a gut feeling

Twenty-six years ago…

"Does your mother dress you, or are you just a queer?" Matt stood there laughing, turning his head to look at Chad.

Chad positioned himself next to Matt. "Probably both," he said, chuckling.

"Leave me alone," Mark lashed out. He got up from the playground bench, walking away with quick, short strides.

"He even walks like a queer," Matt pointed out.

With his back to them, Mark could hear Matt and Chad giggling from behind. The scraping of their sneakers against the unforgiving pavement warned Mark of their pursuit.

"Hey," Matt shouted. "Where are you going? You gonna run back to the teacher like she's your mommy?"

Mark kept walking. Realizing it too late, he found himself distanced from the safety of the other kids and teachers. Out of fear of being isolated, Mark turned to confront his attackers.

"Wow." Matt was surprised. "Maybe Markey boy here does have some balls. You finally going to stick up for yourself?"

"Just stay away from me, boy!" Mark hissed at Matt.

"That's what I thought, pussy. You're all talk. Why don't you do something about it?"

Mark remained silent. He moved in the direction of his classmates, hoping to find refuge among them.

"I don't think so," Matt said, cutting him off. "Why don't you face us like a man? Oh yeah, that's right, because you're a pansy." Mark side-stepped Matt, attempting to avoid his adversary. However, Matt extended his left foot, taking Mark's legs out from under him. Chad maneuvered around the back of Matt and positioned himself on the left side of his friend, attempting to hide the altercation from the nearby kids. "Hold him down," Matt barked.

Chad squatted, holding down Mark's arms with each of his hands and resting his right knee on Mark's chest for added leverage.

"Stop it!" Mark struggled, unable to free himself from the opposing weight.

Matt bent over, lowering his face to Mark. "Shut up, you freak! If the teachers hear you and we get in trouble, you're going to wish you had kept your mouth close."

"Help!" Mark defied Matt's order, praying someone would hear his scream.

Chad, still holding Mark down, twisted his head to look the other way. "I don't think they heard him."

"Well," Matt said, "I guess he's lucky. Unfortunately, he doesn't listen too well, so I'll have to shut him up for good this time." Matt picked up some dirt with his left hand. "Open wide."

Mark continued to resist, his flailing legs proving to be the only defense he could muster.

To avoid his kicking, Matt walked around Chad and kneeled next to Mark's head, out of harm's way. Still holding the dirt, Matt pried Mark's mouth open with his other hand, stuffing the filth deep inside.

Mark began to choke. At the same time, he felt something change profoundly within his body. It was as if all of the fears built up during his elementary years were trying to get out, struggling to fight back. Mark spit out a chunk of the earth previously lodged in his throat. A force, rushing from his gut up through the esophagus, demanded exodus, much like a soul trapped in an unwanted body. Powerless to control his actions, Mark vomited while Matt's eyes widened in horror.

Present day ...

"Hey, stranger. I didn't expect to see you back so soon. How's the leg doing?" Terry Broussard, my boss, stared up at me from his desk.

"Back to normal for the most part," I replied, standing in the doorway to his office. "Remind me never to go undercover as a death row inmate again."

Terry grinned. "I thought you liked playing hero."

"Hero? Yes. Guinea pig? Not so much."

"Well, at least your hair is starting to grow back." Terry chuckled.

I rubbed the fuzz atop my head. "Wouldn't exactly be my top choice next time around. Not that I had an alternative."

"In any event, it's good to have you back. Why don't you take a seat?" He pointed to one of the two chairs in front of his desk.

I leaned against the door frame. "That's okay. I've been sitting for days. I'd prefer to stand if you don't mind."

"Suit yourself." Terry paused temporarily, searching for a paper on his desk. "I've got a couple of things I'd like to discuss with you," he said with the document in his hand.

"You have something for me?"

"As luck would have it. Apparently, a prisoner at Lansing was found dead this morning."

"Natural causes?"

"Unfortunately not," Terry replied. "According to Detective Watts, the scene was pretty disturbing."

"So? We see prison murders on occasion. Cellmates get pissed at one another. No surprise there. Lansing homicide would have jurisdiction in this case."

"Well, that's where it gets interesting."

I squinted. "What do you mean?"

"You're right about jurisdiction. However, you're assuming the culprit was a prisoner."

"You're telling me he wasn't?" I stood upright, Terry piquing my interest.

"A guard," he said. "Zach Johnson."

I raised my eyebrows in disbelief. "You're kidding." Taking a deep breath, I continued. "Even so, why would it involve us?"

"Because he's a fugitive."

"What? How the hell did he escape? The prison would have been on immediate lock down."

"There was another guard doing rounds in the same cell block. He heard the commotion and …"

"Let me guess," I intervened. "He was a witness at the scene and gave his buddy a head start before calling it in."

Terry nodded his head. "Most likely."

"I'm surprised you didn't send Bobby the instant the news broke. He's always the first one in."

"I was about to, but then you walked in," he said with a glimmer in his eye.

"Perfect timing, I suppose." I cracked a smile. "What was the other thing you wanted to discuss."

"He's walking up behind you."

I turned to look. A young man, probably in his late twenties and a good fifteen years younger than me, slowly approached. He owned light brown hair, an Ottoman nose, and full lips. I positioned myself inside Terry's office so he could gain entrance. Decked out in a suite, he glanced at me first, eventually directing his attention toward Terry.

"Uh, hello, sir. I'm…"

"I know who you are son," Terry interrupted. "No need to be nervous." He stood up from his desk, greeting the new arrival. "I'm Chief Deputy Terry Broussard," he said, extending his hand. After making their acquaintance, Terry stared at me, the kid following suit.

"Hi," I said, introducing myself. "Chris Poindexter. Deputy Marshal. Nice to meet you."

"Aydin," he acknowledged. "Aydin Kendell. A pleasure to meet you, sir." He shook my hand.

"You should get going," Terry commented. "Bring Aydin with you."

—

I held open the stairwell door, allowing Aydin to go first. "So, where was home prior to this?"

Aydin smiled at me as he passed, stopping briefly at the top of the stairs to answer my question. "Arlington," he replied.

"Texas or Virginia?" I fell in beside him as the two of us descended the stairs.

"Virginia, sir."

"Everyone comes out of Arlington after their training. I meant where are you from initially? And, by the way, don't even start with the 'sir' thing. Call me Chris, and we'll get along much better," I said, grinning.

"Okay. Thanks, Chris." Aydin paused for a moment. "I'm actually from Arlington. I grew up there and even went to school in the area."

"American University?"

"Uh, no, Georgetown. I received my degree in Biology and applied to the U.S. Marshals Service shortly thereafter."

"Homegrown," I responded. "Nice. What in the world brings you to Topeka?" We reached the parking garage entrance, Aydin securing the door for me this time.

"You, sir. I mean Chris."

"Come again?" I was flabbergasted by his response.

"I heard about your prior case. It made national news. When a position opened up here, I jumped at it."

My shoulders bobbed from laughter. "Seriously?"

Aydin's face, once quiet, turned lighthearted. "Yeah. I know it sounds cheesy, but I want to learn from the best."

"Wow. I'm not sure if I'm embarrassed or flattered, but I appreciate the role model status you've bestowed upon me." I winked at Aydin as we approached my car, pressing a button on the ignition key to unlock the doors.

"So, what's the plan?"

Resting my hands on the roof of the car, I gazed across at him. "I'm gonna drop you at the county morgue on the way to Lansing. The body should be there by now. I'll have a little talk with the prison guard and anyone else who might have been present at the scene."

Aydin and I ducked into the car, fastening our seatbelts. Little did he know, his first day on the job was going to be a long one.

—

"Detective Watts was here earlier," the security guard noted. "I already gave him my statement." The young man sat in a chair across from me, looking away and losing eye contact with me briefly before reconnecting. I noticed a mole, possibly a birth mark, below his right eye as he ran a single hand through his light brown hair.

"I understand that, but the situation has changed now," I responded with a hint of compassion in my voice. He seemed annoyed with me already. "Since your colleague's on the run, it's our jurisdiction now. I just need to ask you some follow-up questions."

"Alright," he said, easing up. "I'm not sure what else I can tell you, though."

I scratched my head. The incoming hair itched, nagging me. "I saw the video surveillance on the way in. Given how old this place is and the lack of new technology, there wasn't much caught on camera. However, it did show your friend running off."

"What's your question?" Impatient, the guard attempted to push things along.

"Actually, I was making a simple observation, but I do have a question. What are the odds of an incident like this occurring in one of the surveillance's blind spots?"

"Honestly?" He tilted his head in thought. "I'm not sure exactly, but as you mentioned, the system is outdated. Coupled with the layout of the prison, there tend to be a lot of gaps in coverage. Plus, this is a minimum security compound, so surveillance is typically limited anyway."

"It makes sense," I commented, nodding my head. "Your profile says you've worked here for seven years?"

"Yes, that's correct."

I noticed the name tag on the guard's chest. It read 'J. Hopkins.' I looked down at his profile again. "Jeffrey."

"Just Jeff," he said huffing.

"Are you okay?" Jeff began to perspire, laboring heavily as he tried to catch his breath. Before he could respond, Jeff keeled over, collapsing onto the floor. I immediately lunged toward the ground, hoping in some way to assist, though my medical background was basic at best. My eyes widened at the sight of his violent convulsing. He required attention, much more than I could provide.

—

Aydin observed the pathologist. Young for a man of his position, the doctor was probably fresh out of school he thought.

"You realize it will be a while before I file the preliminary autopsy report," he said.

"I understand," Aydin replied. "I just want to get your initial thoughts on what the cause of death might have been. It could be useful in our investigation." He hesitated before continuing. "For example, what are those?" Aydin pointed in the direction of the victim's face. White, narrow tubes, almost like giant worms several feet in length, extended from the man's abdomen to the top of his head.

"I can tell you what I think they are, but I'm not sure I can make sense of it myself, so I doubt you will understand."

"You might be surprised," Aydin said, smirking.

"Well, with an open mind and nothing else, I'd say they're Cuvierian tubules."

"What?" Aydin was confused, much to the amusement of the doctor.

"I told you."

Aydin noticed the doctor grinning at him. "No, I'm familiar with Cuvierian tubules," Aydin countered, "but you usually find them inside sea cucumbers. What the heck are they doing on our victim?"

"That's the million dollar question, isn't it?"

"Okay." Aydin pondered. "Aside from the bizarre circumstances, what else do we know?"

"If you're familiar with these tubules, as well as the anatomy of the sea cucumber, you probably realize they release…"

"Holothurin," Aydin interjected.

"Precisely," the doctor continued. "The toxin can affect the nervous system and cause blindness if exposed to the eyes, which was the case with our victim."

"But the toxin has only been shown to cause blindness in humans, not death."

"You're right, but that's based on the low amounts we typically see. These tubules are much longer than normal, which tells me the source is significantly larger than a sea cucumber. The higher quantity could make it lethal to humans. What are you doing?"

"I'm calling my partner. He's going to want to hear this."

—

"He seems to be stable, at least for now." The head prison physician glanced at me, lacking confidence in his voice.

"Any idea what might have brought this on?" Still in minor shock from the guard's earlier episode, I was curious to know.

"It's hard to say until I do further testing. Severe stress can sometimes trigger convulsions, though the source of it is usually due to some other underlying problem."

My cell phone buzzed. The doctor fixed his eyes on me, detecting the noise from where he stood. "I'm sorry," I said, looking down at the vibrating phone. "I'll step outside to take this." Walking out of the medical clinic, I flipped open the console. "Lonely already," I joked.

"Hey, Chris. This is Aydin."

"Yeah, I know. What's up?"

"I've got some interesting information for you," he said, panting.

Based on his short breath and frantic pace of speech, he was worked up over something. "Okay," I said. "Take a second to collect yourself, and tell me what's on your mind."

"Sorry." Aydin took a deep breath and exhaled before continuing. "We don't know the official cause of death yet, but the pathologist was very helpful in coming to some early conclusions."

"Lay it on me, rook."

"Rook?"

"Rookie. Sorry. Carry on."

"Okay. Anyway, do you know what echinoderms are?"

"Echino-what?" The kid was speaking another language to me.

"Echinoderms," he repeated. "You know, starfish, sea urchins, sea cucumbers, stuff like that?"

"Well, now that you put it in English, yes. What, did the guy eat one of them for dinner last night?"

Aydin chuckled. "Not quite. Instead, he had the digestive tract from one of them, a sea cucumber to be exact, tangled around the upper half of his body."

"What?" *Is this kid on crack or something?*

"As a defense mechanism, sea cucumbers will sometimes release Cuvierian tubules, which are worm-like tentacles found in their digestive system."

"Are these tentacles poisonous?"

"How'd you know?" Aydin sounded surprised.

"I didn't," I replied. "It was a guess based on where you seem to be going with this."

"They release a toxin called Holothurin. It can mess with the central nervous system and cause death at high doses."

I took a few seconds to let all of it soak in. "Okay, so our fugitive must have gotten his hands on one of these things, knowing what they can do, and unleashed it on our victim, who just happened to piss him off."

"A good theory," Aydin noted, "but there's one problem."

"What's that?"

"Tubules from a sea cucumber wouldn't kill a human. The toxin can cause blindness if exposed to the eyes, but it's not concentrated enough to be lethal. These tubules were several feet long and held the toxin in much higher quantities. If our prisoner died from this, it had to come from something a lot bigger."

Shit.

"Are you still there?" Aydin inquired.

"Yeah, I'm still here. I'm just thinking about how fucked up this day is getting."

—

"You never told me over the phone. How did your interview with the other guard go?" Aydin gawked at me from the passenger seat.

"I've had better conversations before."

"What does that mean?" Aydin interjected before I could continue.

I exhaled. "The guy fell into an epileptic state shortly after, so I didn't get much out of him."

"Holy…" Aydin refrained from cursing. "Really?"

"Yeah, he was convulsing on the floor in front of me. I didn't know what to do, so I called for one of the prison doctors."

"Is he okay?"

"Come on!" I laid on the horn. Aydin twisted his head to look, quickly diverting his attention back to me. "That jerk just cut me off," I remarked.

"It happens." He brushed it off as if it were nothing, displaying more curiosity for my answer.

"He was stable when I left but still unconscious." A notion popped into my head as I said it. "Hey."

"Yeah."

"Is it possible the guard was exposed to the same toxin as the victim?"

"I suppose. He was obviously at the scene. Did he show any signs of this when you talked to him?"

"You mean, was he wearing a bunch of tentacles on his shirt?"

Aydin giggled and smiled. "Something like that."

"No, but if toxin was released on the victim, there's a chance he was exposed through cross-contamination."

"It's possible," Aydin commented. "It would make sense given the fact he didn't die. Maybe he was exposed at a much smaller level."

A call was coming in on my dashboard phone. "Probably Terry," I said, hitting the speaker button.

"Chris. It's Terry."

Grinning, I winked at Aydin. "What's up, boss?"

"We've got a location on our fugitive. According to one of our confidential informants, he's holed up in a trailer park just south of Leavenworth. A friend's place apparently. I have a team in route, but you guys are closer. Can you and Aydin do a one-eighty and head up there?"

"What do you want us to do?" I asked.

"Just stake the place out until we get there," Terry replied. "If he leaves, follow him, but don't approach him until back-up has arrived. Stay in touch, and keep us abreast of any developments."

"On our way." I looked over at Aydin as I terminated the connection. "Ready for another road trip, kid?" Though he failed to answer, his mischievous look told me everything.

—

"You sure that's the one?" Aydin looked in the direction of the beaten down trailer home.

"What does the number read on the mailbox?" I dropped my head to glance at the cell phone.

"One-one-four-zero," he said.

"That's it. The number matches the street address Terry texted me." I killed the ignition, picking up a cup of coffee from the beverage holder positioned between Aydin and me. "You should have gotten some." I took a sip. The coffee was still hot.

Aydin shook his head. "I've never been much of a coffee drinker."

"You sound like me twenty years ago. I was the same way. Now I can't live without it. You'll learn, though. I'll bet you one-hundred dollars you're drinking coffee before the year is up."

He snickered. "Anything's possible, so I won't call you on that one."

"Smart kid. Just don't tell Terry about this. I'd get an earful if he knew we stopped off for coffee on the way to a stakeout."

"How long until they get here?"

"Well, we were about halfway to Topeka when we made the U-turn. That would put them about 30 minutes behind us."

"But we stopped for coffee," Aydin commented with a smirk on his face.

"Good point, so I would say they're fifteen to twenty minutes out. It will give us some time to look over this guy's profile."

"You think we're positioned okay here?" Aydin raised a legitimate concern.

"We're about thirty yards from the trailer, and based on the angle of the house, I imagine it's hard to get a clear view of us from any of the windows. I think we're good. Plus, we can see both the front and back yard from here."

"What do we know about this guy?"

Putting my coffee down, I grabbed the file from the dash. "Zach Johnson," I noted, opening the folder. "He's only been at Lansing for a few months. It says he lives with his mother. Kind of strange for a guy who's thirty-eight, but not unheard of."

"We're assuming he's in there. He could have bailed before we even got here."

"True, but until we know otherwise, we sit tight."

Aydin grabbed another folder from the dash. As he perused the file, something caught his attention. "This Hopkins guy…"

"Jeff," I interrupted.

"Yeah. Based on his statement, he didn't witness the murder. Supposedly, he heard the commotion and arrived on the scene after the fact."

"That's right. Terry mentioned it to me this morning. We already knew that, so what's your point?"

"No point really. I guess I'm disappointed we didn't get more out of this guy. What did he say about the description of the victim?"

"It should be right there in front of you. If I remember correctly, though, he pretty much confirmed what you and the pathologist saw. He couldn't explain it, but the description seems to match up."

"But you said our fugitive, Zach, has only been at Lansing for a few months. Right?"

I nodded my head.

"If that's the case, Zach and Jeff hardly knew each other. Why would Jeff cover for him?"

"Are you kidding?" I was surprised by Aydin's comments. "First of all, you're assuming they didn't know each other that well. If Zach is living with his mother, you have to wonder just how many friends he has. Maybe he reached out to Jeff, and the two of them hit it off. It doesn't take long to form a connection in some cases. Also, just like there's a code between prisoners, there's a code between guards. You don't give up one of your own."

"It makes sense," Aydin said. "However, in the end, Jeff did give him up."

"Technically, you're right."

There was a tap at the window.

"Jesus!" I jumped back in my seat, startled from the noise. "Bobby," I said with relief in my voice as I lowered the window. "You could have called or reached me on the CB."

He laughed. "Where would the fun be in that? You two ready?"

—

Bobby approached the trailer from the back, while Aydin and I made for the front door. As protocol, the three of us wore Kevlar vests under our windbreaker jackets. We were also equipped with ear pieces, keeping us in constant contact with one another. A fourth team member, who made the trip with Bobby, was obscured in a vacant lot across the street. His sniper abilities usually came in handy, giving us an added sense of security.

"Remember," I whispered to Aydin. "I go in first, and you bring up the rear once it's clear."

He nodded his head.

"We don't know how many people are in there," I added. "We're assuming two, including our man, but it could be more."

"Got it," Aydin replied.

Even though it was early November, strands of holiday lights already dangled from the overhang of the sky blue trailer. I took a deep breath and exhaled, gripping the Glock 22 semi-automatic pistol in my right hand. Aydin held his with both hands, keeping the gun out in front of him. "U.S. Marshals Service!" I barked out while banging the door with my left hand. Taking a step back, I extended my right leg and propelled it toward the door, hitting the fragile aluminum frame with immense force. Despite being an out swinging door, I managed to dislocate the frame from its hinges.

Zach was situated on the couch directly in front of me. "Stay where you are, Mr. Johnson," I commanded with my gun pointing at him. There was a hallway to my left. I glanced briefly to make sure no one was making a surprise run at me. Out of my peripheral vision, a blur appeared. Zach peeled off toward the back of the trailer. "Shit. Bobby, he's coming your way."

"Roger," Bobby answered.

Intending to pursue Zach, I remembered about Aydin. As I turned to face him, a gentleman streaked from one of the hallway bedrooms. The man, probably the owner, was at the front door and on top of Aydin before he even knew what hit him. "Freeze," I screamed, holding my gun with both hands, hesitating to shoot given his proximity to Aydin. He bowled over Aydin, knocking him to the ground. Exiting the trailer, my first concern was for my partner.

"You have him, A.J.?"

"Got'em in my scope," he said. "He's not going anywhere."

Bending down to check on Aydin, I heard the blast of the sniper rifle in the distance. The guy hightailing it away from us fell to the ground as A.J. put a bullet in his leg. I closed on him before he could get up.

"Stay down," I roared, placing my left leg on his back. "Hands behind your head." Holstering my gun, I whipped out the handcuffs, tightening and securing them around his wrists. Aydin was at my side brushing himself off. "You okay?"

"Yeah."

"Watch him," I said, "while I go check on Bobby."

"Sure thing." Aydin, a little shaken and embarrassed, stood there with his pistol aimed at the ground.

Running around the back corner of the trailer, I spotted Bobby. Zach laid face down on the ground, Bobby's 12-gauge shotgun pointing in his direction.

"Please, I didn't do anything," Zach pleaded. "He told me to run, to make it look like I did it. If I didn't do what he said, he threatened to kill my mom. Please, you have to believe me."

"Christ," I murmured to myself. "We have the wrong guy."

—

"We're on our way," I said. "We're about five minutes out." Disconnecting the call, I stepped on the gas pedal.

"Where is he?" Aydin referred to Jeff when posing the question.

"On the run, unfortunately. After waking up from his little nap, he knocked the doctor unconscious and left as if he was going home. It was the end of his shift, so no one questioned his actions. Everyone was unaware of the situation until now."

"So, where are we headed?"

"His parents' house," I acknowledged. "Marshals combed his residence, but there was no sign of him. His parents live close by, so it's worth a shot."

Aydin examined Jeff's file again. "These files are pretty amazing," he noted.

"Why's that?"

"The information," he commented. "It dates all the way back to his childhood. I'm conscious of our intel methods, but it's still incredible when you think about it."

"Tax dollars at work," I replied. "If you have enough resources, you can dig up just about anything."

"Hmm." Aydin scratched his chin.

"What is it?"

"According to school records, Jeff was out of school for several weeks during the fifth grade."

"So? Do they give a reason?" I inquired, still unclear what Aydin was getting at.

"Just says it was due to an undisclosed illness."

Staring at Aydin, I could tell he was in thought. "Okay. Spill it already."

"I might be taking a big leap here, but what if Jeff wasn't exposed to the toxin after all? What if he's the actual carrier?"

"In what way?" Things were getting weird again.

"In the sense that the Cuvierian tubules, or tentacles as you like to call them, came from Jeff."

"How is that even possible? You said yourself these things only come from sea…" I paused trying to think of the word.

"Cucumbers," Aydin said, finishing my sentence. "I did, but the pathologist said the tubules would have had to come from something much bigger given their size, as well as the large dosage of Holothurin."

"Are you expecting me to believe this guy is some combination of human and sea creature?"

"I don't know what to think. What I do know, however, is that sea cucumbers usually require a few weeks of down time to regenerate the lost portion of their digestive system. It could be why Jeff had such a long absence from school and why he keeled over during your briefing. Maybe this has happened to him before."

"You realize how crazy this shit sounds, right?" I was uncertain whether to keep an open mind or be pissed at him for concocting such a story. I shook my head. "Assuming I can somehow grasp this concept, where does it leave us?"

"Well, for one thing, he shouldn't be able to use this defense mechanism against us given his need to regenerate."

"That's good," I commented. "If even half of what you're saying is true, it could give us an advantage." I hit the brakes, slowing the car to a complete stop. "This is it."

Bobby and A.J. pulled up behind us, quickly departing the car. A.J. removed a shotgun from the trunk, leaving his regular sniper rifle behind. He was in charge of covering the back this time around. Bobby, also carrying a shotgun, took the lead as Aydin and I fell in behind him. Walking up the concrete driveway, I observed the Tudor-style home. Light blue in color with white trim around the windows, the house was soft on the eyes. Before Bobby even made it up the steps, the front door swung open. Gray stones, mounted along the exterior wall, surrounded the door's frame. A woman appeared.

"Whoa," Bobby yelled, raising his shotgun. "Hold it right there, ma'am."

The woman trembled. "Please don't hurt my son," she begged with her hands in the air.

"I need you to slowly step outside, Mrs. Hopkins," Bobby ordered. "Keep your hands where they are, so I can see them."

She obliged, turning to look back as she stepped forward. Bobby grabbed her.

"Is your son in the house, ma'am?" I took the lead with Aydin close behind me.

"He's not going to hurt anyone," she replied. "He's just resting. He isn't well."

"Is your husband here?" I wanted to get a head count to make sure there were no surprises.

"No. He's at work. It's just me and Mark, or Jeffery as you probably know him by."

Bobby cuffed her, gently lowering her to the ground. She kneeled in the front yard, hands behind her back.

"He didn't mean to do it," she screamed as Aydin and I entered the house. "He can't help it!" Making our way deeper into the house, her voice trailed off.

The hallway opened into a large living area. Jeff was curled up in the back corner of the room, partially obstructed by the rocking chair beside him. He shivered, seemingly weak and in poor health. Wearing street clothes and showing no signs of a weapon, Jeff appeared harmless. However, as with any situation, I erred on the side of caution and kept my pistol pointed at him. Aydin brushed my shoulder, slowly walking past me.

"Wait," I whispered.

Aydin put his left hand out, attempting to calm my fears. He holstered his gun to avoid showing any aggression towards Jeff. "Hi, Jeff," he said with a soothing voice. "I know you're scared, and you're not feeling well. We're not here to hurt you. We just want to help." Jeff glanced at Aydin, remaining in a fetal position like a little kid too scared to come out from his hiding place. "It's okay," Aydin continued in a calming manner. "It wasn't your fault. You didn't mean to do it. Right? Jeff shook his head. "Tell you what. It's our job, so we have to take you with us, but we'll make sure you get all of the medical attention you need. Okay?" He nodded again.

I moved in to help Jeff up, Aydin doing the honor of cuffing him once he got to his feet. Given his feeble condition, Jeff leaned against Aydin as we escorted him down the hallway.

"Ah!" It sounded like Bobby.

"Stay with Jeff," I said, hauling ass toward the front door. "A.J., move in to assist Aydin." I spoke through my ear piece while exiting the house. *Holy Shit*. I had to do a double-take based on what I was witnessing. White tentacles hung from Mrs. Hopkins' mouth, gradually making their way toward Bobby's leg.

"What the hell," Bobby yelled, pointing his shotgun at her head.

"No, don't," I pleaded. Thinking swiftly, I grasped the taser gun on the other side of my holster and fired two electrodes into her abdomen. She winced from the uncontrolled muscle movement, temporarily halting her advancement.

Bobby threw her to the ground face first, helping keep the danger at bay until he could gag her. "Get some duct tape from the car," he said, motioning to A.J.

Aydin stepped outside and made his way to our car, securing Jeff in the back seat. Holstering my taser gun, I approached the rookie with a smile. "Wow," I said. "I'm impressed. Nice job in there."

"Thanks," Aydin replied, grinning. "I like to think of myself as the smart one."

"Smart ass, maybe." I chuckled, placing my hand on his shoulder. "Seriously, though, not bad for your first day."

"So, that was quite the surprise back there."

"No shit. I guess it's safe to say Jeff's problem runs in the family."

"Really?" Aydin joked. "Are you basing that on fact, or is it just a gut feeling of yours? Plenty of pun intended," he noted.

The two of us laughed together.

skylar da vinci

Hey, my name's Skylar and I am what people call a young writer. I've been writing ever since I was 10, and now I'm 13 years old. Most of my writing or poetry falls into the genres of horror, sci-fi, or supernatural. I enjoy writing because it breaks the restraints on my creativity. Writing helps me paint a mental picture in the reader's mind.

I write about a person, usually inhuman, who is running or trying to escape from the place that has held them captive. Some of my other stories involve a person who was hurt by someone in the past, and she was able to escape from them. She was free from this person until she was captured and he saved her.

I write stories and poetry, but I'm also an artist. I think the artistic side of me allows me to be able to describe someone or something better. I started drawing before
I became a writer, and I began to write poetry only a few months ago. I get inspired by most of the books I read, like Maximum Ride, and they help me learn to fix my mistakes in my writing. Like I said, writing breaks my creativity free. It allows my mind to enter different worlds that I would have never been able to even dream of before.

broken freedom

I stare at the fiery scene
As billows of ash enter the sky
Ruins of a city surround me
Blocking every exit
Not a single soul has survived
Only I remain
They all opened their hands
But were betrayed
I take a step
And lick my lips
The air has turned cold
Even with the neverending flame
I can see a mirror
Reflecting my every emotion
I want to run
I want to escape
But my freedom was taken
When this apocalypse began
I cannot leave
I cannot remove myself
From this broken picture
I can only watch
As my people perish
I can only listen to their screams

I smell their burning flesh
As if it were painted into my senses
I see their pain
They reach for me
But I cannot help them
I will only do what has already been done
I will not look
Into their hopeful eyes
I will not listen
As they beg for mercy
The fire extends its hands
Almost like claws
I feel the heat
As if the Sun God were by my side
I cringe and step back
I stare at the gaunt face of Death
And stop
I have only one fate in this world
The fate has already been chosen
I have no say
I have no word
This was sealed the day I was born
Death came foward,
Its eyes like blood
I stand tall
I stand without a hint of fear
But deep within
I wish for freedom
The smoke wraps around me
Like a blanket of Death

It enters my lungs
Sucking away my breath
I gasp for air
But it does not return
My life is slowly draining
But I will not leave
My soul will remain
In this broken world
I feel them watching me
I feel their eyes
I fall to my knees
And look down
Ash stains my cloak
Flames grip my flesh
I feel Death's claw grasping my neck
I keep my head low
And my eyes closed
This demon will not win
I won't allow it
Though my shell may be broken
I shall remain
I shall haunt them until
The end of time

falling

I can see the ground
It's coming to fast
I can feel the wind
Nipping at my face
Pain vibrates throughout
Like a neverending flame
The world has stopped
But I'm still falling
No one sees me
No one hears my screams
And if they did
They wouldn't help
I reach for something
But it isn't there
I close my eyes
And wait for the end
I can feel the trees brush against my arms
I can smell the freshly cut grass
It's overwhelming
How so many people can stand this
Every day?
The pain numbs
But fear takes its place
My soul shatters
As I fall
The ground is too close
Close enough to touch

I make contact
But feel no pain
I open my eyes
And see the midnight sky
Stars come into view
Almost like a million lights
I listen to the sound
Of my rapid heartbeat
And the sound of the trees
As they dance in the wind
To a silent song
I wait
But no one comes
No one helps the fallen soul
They leave me lying
In the grass
I feel like a shadow
Waiting to be released
I close my eyes
And allow myself
To fall

the light

Her eyes scan the crowd
Searching for something unknown
Not a single person looks at her
Because they don't care
She steps foward
Fear in every step
Her head lifts towards the sky
Where a glowing light has appeared
No one else looks up
They only pass
The strange girl
As she stares into the night
The light grows brighter
Stronger
Its rays mimicking the sun
A few people look up in wonder
But she doesn't care
Others stop and stare
But she doesn't move
The light moves closer
Gravitating towards her
She is like a powerful magnet
An interesting sight
The air turns cold
The trees fall foward
Ocean waves
Crash into the shore

She stands there
Like a concrete statue
Her eyes fall onto the light
As it drifts towards her
People stare in suprise
At the sight of this almost
Impossibly scene
The girl steps foward
Her pale fingers moving
Ever so slightly
The wind tugs at her long hair
Extending it like a shadow
Everyone watches
Their heads shaking
It seems almost unreal
That this light becomes human
She stands there
Her eyes unfocused
Dead
The wind stills
The Earth comes to a halt
Time has been frozen
No one moves
No one but the light
It takes a step forward
Watching her
Waiting
She moves
Moves towards him
Her eyes open

Skylar Da Vinci

The light reaches for her
But she doesn't follow
Her eyes flicker
Flicker evil
A scream erupts
The people are on their knees
Crimson blood falls like tears
Down their shocked faces
The girl smiles
A smile worthy of the Cheshire Cat
The light cringes
Its hand shakes like a leaf
Her eyes dance across the ground
Into the sky
She grabs something
Air
It whips around her
Through her hair
Across her arms
The light slowly begins to disappear
Its glowing light dims
The shaking hand pulls forward
But it is never taken
The girl takes a step
Its sound almost ear shattering
The wind changes
Its speed increases
Now moving as fast
As a jet plane
It grabs the light
Embraces it

But the grasp burns
It hurts the light
The scream returns
But she doesn't listen
Her eyes just watch
Watch until the light falls back
Its breath becomes gasps
As the light searches for air
She turns to face the crowd
Everyone is watching her
The girl brushes past humans
Her eyes stay open
As the screams turn to silence
And the light is forever taken
By Darkness

shelley koon

Shelley Koon portrait by Minix

Shelley Koon is an artist and writer currently residing in the San Francisco Bay Area. She enjoys horseback riding, long walks in the rain, kittens, puppies and killing, dismembering and disfiguring people in Adobe Photoshop, Microsoft Word and several popular MMOs.

http://twitter.com/shelleykoon

http://www.facebook.com/pages/Shelley-Koon/194046663991798

http://shelleykoon.com/author/

https://plus.google.com/112678186134740033778

anasazi

Shelley Koon

the hive

torn kaos

while it sleeps

numb

stuti jain

I don't write stories, I write dreams, and my stories are somehow a reflection of my life and inner self. People wish if it were possible to re-write the past, I live that wish through my stories.

This story is about a young guy, who is passionately in love with his would be wife, but somehow, he cannot leave the girl who still owned him despite being away from him. This story is a turbulence of emotions and also a question to my readers, what will you do when your love returns in your life?

i love you too

"No! I don't want to; you've always been so cold, stone heart-"

"And you, you've always melted this stone hearted person to an extent he can never explain."

The rest of Sharon's words were drowned by the smooth brushing of the passionate lips that were determinately grasping her trembling ones. She was never able to resist the handsome monster who was so insistent on battering her senses to a sweet defeat. Had he been so ardent in really loving her and understanding her, she would have been a lot better. Sharon pondered. Four years is a quite long time! God! How time flew away. It seemed as if it were yesterday when they went out for their first date. Sharon knew he could drive her crazy no matter how angry or upset she was with him. A first rate philanderer! She smiled, one who could seduce the *Aphrodite* herself! Those big, beautiful brown eyes with heavy eyelashes, captivating smile that possessed the entire enigma to bewitch any girl on earth, those strong manly muscles, no girl alive on Earth in her right senses could have ever resisted. Sharon beamed with happiness. And he, he had chosen her above all the other women in the world to chain her forever in his arms. It was impossible for her at times to believe that he really loved her and that too, to such an extent. It was unbelievable. And if he really did why was he so intimate and reserved at times even with her as if she was some third person and not his lover.

"Are you still trying to recover from the shock of what we just did *or* are you thinking about some innovative ways to kiss?"

There was a mischievous look in his eyes.

"Nothing of the two actually, but yes, I was thinking over innovative ways to-"

"Kissing!" He supplied.

"No! To butcher you into pieces for doing this to me"

"What? Kissing?" He looked into her eyes.

"You guys have nothing else on your minds. Isn't it?" Sharon smiled.

"If you ask me there are a great lot of things on my mind besides just kissing but I dare not tell them to you, now."

"Not now? Then when?"

"Later. At the right time and at right place." Sharon gave a meaningful nod, blushing.

They laughed in unison and finally bade each other *au revoir* with a warm hug. The memories of all the beautiful moments spent with Justin came hovering over Sharon's mind until she drowned herself into them to a pleasant sleep on the grandesque chaise longe that had also been one of his gifts to her. She loved interiors and décor, and Justin knew it just too well.

chapter 2: the surprise

Clad in a square, low cut, black evening gown with a narrow vee tapered at the back, Sharon decided to wear her hair down but it looked too ornate. So she rather decided to tie back her blond hair in a neat, sophisticated bun and hung the tendrils on the front loose like grapevine to concentrate on her pear shaped, beautiful face.

A light pink, or perhaps a mauve shade, would be perfect for the evening but then applied a crimson shade instead. She had worn heavy diamond earrings, with a ruby in the center of each. She liked them a lot—no—loved them, Sharon corrected with a smile. She was looking perfect for the evening. He would be here any moment. She could even feel him, looking into her deep brown eyes; she could feel something happening to her, she closed her eyes and enjoyed the moment to feel his protective arms around her.

"Sharon ! Are you ready baby? I already came ten minutes late. By habit I know you women can never be ready on time, there's always something that you forget and- "

God! He gaped how beautiful she looked! He was speechless.

"You look beautiful!" he meant it.

Sharon looked at Justin, her cheeks all roses. Justin was a sweetheart and today clad in a blue tunic he could give serious competition to the Adonis himself!

Taking her hand into his' and kissing it he led her to the brand new Rolls Royce he had just got.

"Do you like our new car? Sharon.. Chaillet?"

Sharon Chaillet! Her name sounded so beautiful with his name. Sharon was completely ecstatic; there was moisture in her eyes. Justin pressed a brief, warm kiss on her neck completely forgetting that they were in a chauffeur driven cab who saw everything in the rear view mirror on the front.

The car stopped before a beautiful house, no, A Palace! Sharon was taken aback.

"Oh Christ! Is this Heaven?" she blurted.

"Not yet! But we'll make it together, soon." Justin bit his lip. Sharon was a masterpiece of God, a stunning, beautiful blond who always tantalized his senses, someone who could make the heads turn around. She wore perfect make up which accentuated her beauty even more. The sparks within her eyes had started to burn him already. She had a fire within herself. She had all, dreams, desires, ambitions, beauty and intelligence and yet she was never off ground. Justin had always loved her and her vulnerability. He had always wanted to protect her, to love her, to care for her and the most important of all to have her, to possess all of her charm, beauty and intelligence and that rich, determinant fire that had started to show sparks of life. She was so tender and so full of life. He was proud of her.

They entered into a large hall which consisted of long staircase in marble. The whole interior of the house was in satin green and gold. The paintings on the walls were also golden bordered and bore the sophisticated Italian touches. Each of them was exquisite and rare. The glass on the windows too, was shimmering of the hues of golden. There was a large sofa, again in dark green and golden. The huge dining table that Justin had brought from Paris, two years back also lay there with expensive crockery from Italy itself.

The dinner had already been prepared. The servants served the dinner. There was everything from soupe de courgettes, tagliatelles à la saucisse, crème renversées à la banane, Truites en gratin de pain d'épices, choucroute, le cèpe, tarte tatin aux zestes d'oranges to Ananas en carpaccio et coriandre cristallisée. Justin took pride in being French and he loved every part of it from food to culture. Thanks to his cosmopolitan business Justin spoke English fluently. Sharon was in the States when they met and finally they were together in New York. Justin had to manage his family business which was being run from New York and Sharon pursued an MBA from the New York University. She had always regretted not knowing his native language. This was the time she could make up for all of it.

"Bon Apétit Chéri!" she wished with confidence brimming not in her smile but, her eyes as well.

"What? I thought you spoke-"

"French!" Sharon supplied for him.

"Oui ! Je l'ai appris pour toi ! Il y a deux mois", Sharon beamed.

"I Love you!", is all Justin managed to say.

A mischievous smile lurked upon his face as he looked at Sharon.

"By the way, has my last meeting with Isabella got to do anything with you learning French?"

Justin was peeping into her gay eyes. He could still feel the twang of jealousy in them.

"Partly that and partly for you…" she trailed off.

Isabella was Justin's ex-girlfriend. She was also French like him and Sharon still fell hurt as she remembered the intensity of love-affair Justin had with Isabella. They always talked in French over the phone and internet till Sharon finally came to know about it. Justin had claimed her to be a close friend which he had clarified later and asked forgivness for. Since then, Sharon had been regularly checking his mails which were mostly in French. She used a translator to help make sense of them.

"It's a matter of the past sweetheart. I was quite young then. I was attracted towards her though I was never in love with her. Isabella knew that too. It is *you* who I'm in love with," Justin explained to Sharon who was looking pensive.

Sharon trusted him. She knew he would never cheat upon her but then his secrecy sometimes perturbed her. Why did he become so unusually quiet at times, after a relationship of four years it was still a mystery for Sharon. She did not notice when Justin got up from his place and came near her.

"I'm yours, only yours, forever! It's you my heart craves for," Justin put his hands around her shoulders.

Sharon hugged him. It had been a good day.

After the dinner they talked until midnight. They talked about Justin's new business ventures, Sharon's new friends who envied her for her marvelous jewelry and dresses, their first date and so on. Sharon was a complete chatter box who always had some or the other topic for discussion. Justin loved her innocence and naiveté. She was like a small at times trying to impress her copains. Justin was marveled at how she could change one topic to another and then quickly came back to the original one. He always forgot the whereabouts of the topic he wanted to discuss with her, when she started speaking. Still he always admired her company though he generally felt the need of an Aspirin after a long discussion with her.

The two fell asleep next to each other.

It was around two at night when Justin woke up. Sharon was sleeping on the couch, curled up like an infant. His angel was sleeping sound even on that uncomfortable couch. She looked so peaceful that Justin had the sudden urge to pull her into his arms. He took her in his arms, carried her off safely to the bedroom, and laid her down on the soft bed. He then turned off the lights after pressing a warm kiss on her forehead and headed for the guestroom himself.

Love can be so amusing at times, he thought. He was sleeping in the guestroom of his own mansion for her, who was sleeping on his own bed, in his bedroom, and whom he dearly loved. He smiled and went off to sleep.

chapter 3: the letter

Sharon was surprised to wake up alone in the bed. Where was Justin, she thought. She got up from the bed and realized that she was not in the same room as last night. She opened the door and walked down the stairs.

"Good Morning Madam, Mr. Chaillet has already left for office. He wanted you to call him after you have had your breakfast," a middle aged servant informed her.

"Alright! Where can I take a bath?" Sharon asked looking around the huge place. It looked more beautiful in the day light she noticed.

"Miss Lebroy will assist you in five minutes. I'll send her away to your room," Edroua, the household servant provided.

Sharon smiled. Justin had taken care of everything and instructed all the servants beforehand. Idol of Practicality!

Having bathed and put away her worn clothes. The petite housemaid had taken out for her a new wardrobe from the large armoire that had all the clothing a girl could ever think of. Sharon was gleaming with happiness. Justin was too good at surprises.

She had her breakfast and then called up Justin like an obedient girl. The telecaller hung her for five minutes on the *line when he was finally there.*

"Morning! So? Did you sleep well honey?"

"Oh Justin! It was awesome; you had planned everything right from my room to my wardrobe?"

"You like it?"

"I Love it! The collection is fabulous. You never told me you're doing all this."

"You never let me speak and even if I tried I would get lost among your talks. Moreover, I want this to be a surprise for you."

"Well, how many surprises have you planned? Huh? First the car, then the house, then the collection, is there more? Please don't, I'll die out of happiness."

Justin laughed.

"You had breakfast?"

"Yep! And you?"

"Not yet, you know, lots of work but don't worry, we'll have lunch together. I'll come to pick you up at 2. Be ready on time. Till then complete your presentations. Bye!"

Sharon had completely forgotten about the presentations, she had to complete them by Friday. It was already Wednesday, and she had not even begun. She called up her friend Nathalie and discussed the topic of her presentation.

The two friends though being the exact opposites of each other in nature and believes were alike in one respect, even Nathalie had not begun with the presentation. Though she took notes on the same regularly.

Sharon put the phone down with Nathalie promising her to send the notes via E-mail while she headed for Justin's study to find some papers and pens to prepare some notes herself.

She opened up the drawers of the antique ebony table. There lay a huge pile of boring files in it. She opened up the second drawer which was again loaded with files. She opened the third one to find a diary with a pen in it. She took it and opened it.

It looked like a personal diary where you wrote your daily routine in. She flipped through the pages and suddenly stopped at one, in which there was a dry rose. She read-

13 December, 1992

I had never been happier in my entire life. Even mom was exuberant. Dad had given his consent after all the melodrama. We had done it after all. I owe it to you darling. But the funniest thing of all is that no one knows till now that we have already done it. I told my mom about the sapphire ring I had got for you after saving months of my pocket-money. She could not believe I actually did that. After all I'm just 18 and you know what guys of my age are up to at the age of 18. Booze parties, sex, drugs and what not. Like all my friends, she too finally put forward the conclusion of me being too much in love. They just don't know about the havoc you create on me. It's above all those things a guy generally desires for. I miss your soft kisses and passionate hugs. Had Dad not made me swear, not to meet until our D-day, I would have flown to your arms, the place where I find the ultimate bliss. I love you so much! This time-span is killing me, torturing me. But I know it will be well paid off when I will be with you, when we will be together, at last!

Sharon swooned. He had been in love? Sapphire ring! Hugs and kisses! She felt torn apart. Who was she?

"Isabella!" her mind spoke. But he had swore he was only attracted to her and did not love her. There were huge tears in her eyes. Her mind kept thinking, What had they done? What did he mean by *D-day*? His mom was exuberant and thus, she already knew about it. What does all this mean? What did the dry rose convey?

Sharon felt the fine hammering of her heart into pieces. Her hand and feet were all cold and numb. She could feel something chilling and bitter from inside. 1992! He met her exactly seven years after all this. They had already celebrated four beautiful years of their relationship. It was a long time back but Sharon could not digest the bitter truth that he had been in love with someone else before her. She cried and wept till her eyes were swollen and red. She loved Justin and could not even think of sharing him with someone else. Obviously it seemed foolish to think of this now but for Sharon it was an agony just to realize that the love he had been giving to her, had also be experienced by someone else, someone Justin had never told her about. Justin had told her everything about himself but this. What was the reason that he had hidden this truth from her?

Sharon remembered the look in his eyes whenever he looked at her. They were always inviting and full of love, so full of concern for her. But still she could always feel the strange loneliness in his eyes at times. She never understood the reason for it, neither did she ever understand the strangely reserved composure that he adopted at times even with her. She felt slapped for being deprived of the infernal truth. She did not even get ready for lunch. She was in no mood of a lunch. She felt cheated by the man whom she loved the most in her life. The man for whom she had left her family, three precious years of her career, her hometown, everything: she had sacrificed all for him. And one day the very same girl comes to know that her ardent lover had been intensely in love with someone and for some reason that she did not know yet, decided to hide it from her.

chapter 4: florence

Beep-Beep , Justin pressed hard the horn, once again. It cost him so much to cancel his appointments to be out with Sharon. He had already told her to be ready on time. And as usual, he came late again to assure she was ready on time, but as evident she was not.

"Damn it! Sharon, you're still not ready? Sharon I cancelled my meeting just to-"

Sharon looked up at him straight in his eyes with hers red, swollen and protruding. There were dark circles below them. Justin was horrified to see her in this state.

"Are you alright? What happened? Did anyone say anything to you? Speak-up! Your silence is killing me! Shall I call a doctor?"

"Fuck off Justin! You're a liar! I hate you!"

"What? Liar? When did I lie to you?"

"You did! You hid the truth from me! I never hid anything from you… but you did!"

"Sharon what are you talking about? I've never lied to you, I swear. What have I hidden from you?"

"Ask yourself! Do I know everything about you?"

"Sharon can we discuss this calmly? What are you trying to say?"

"I don't want to discuss anything. You said you were only attracted to her, you lied!"

"Who are you talking about?"

"Isabella!"

"I don't know what made you think I lied to you. It was a matter of past and you know that. She used to be a close friend, I was-"

"Enough Justin! For how many close friends have you bought a sapphire ring out of your own pocket money?"

Justin did not speak a word. The memories of those long walks in the park, those evening balls and finally that church flashed across his mind.

"Are you counting the number of friends for whom you did exactly that? Or for whom you wrote something like this!"

Sharon threw the ominous diary right on his face. She did not notice the tightening of his muscle in his jaw.

"How dare you touch my diary without my permission?"

"Permission? Oh yes! Permission! Did you ever take my permission before kissing me or touching me? Did you ever take my permission before taking me into your arms or your bed?"

That was it. Justin slapped her hard on the face. Sharon burst into tears and flew to her room only to collect her bag and leave immediately for her own flat, crying. Justin still stood there like a statue. He then stood up, went into his study, where Sharon had found his diary.

bradley mcdevitt

Bradley K. McDevitt is a twenty-two year veteran of the gaming industry, and has worked for numerous companies such as WoTC/TSR, Goodman Games, Catalyst Games Lab, Atlas Games and many more. This is not even counting his stints as a staff artist for GDW and as an Art Director for Dark Skull Studios.

At last count, he had over 470 published credits, with over a twenty more in process as of this writing. To old-time gamers, he is best known as the author of cult-favorites It Came From the Late, Late, Late Show and NightLife, as well as Haiiiii-Ya! for Goodman Games.

He likes to re-invent himself as an artist periodically, from beginning an aspiring cartoonist, to currently working in a fusion style of inks and paints, with frequent diversions into digital work and graphic design. He is constantly trying to expand his repertoire of styles, feeling that too much comfort in a single artistic style leads to stagnation and burn-out.

He lives in Tontogany, Ohio with his wife and occasional collaborator, Jessie. In his spare time, he likes to surf the web, explore new musical styles, and watch sci-fi and horror movies.

He may be reached at bkmcdevitt@Yahoo.com and his website is at www.bradleykmcdevitt.net. Further, he may be found on Facebook, Google+ and Artorder.com by that name.

feral faerie

demonic pact

werewolf woman

banshee

autopsy

kc hunter

The writer and creator of the dark fantasy series Paris and the children's series Dorian Delmontez™.

KC Hunter has been a storyteller since he was twelve-years-old, and through various media during his life, been telling them ever since. He won a National Young Writers Award in 1994 and had several poems published in his teen years.

He later delved into music, live performance and interactive media development, but still continued to write through the early 2000s.

In 2008, he developed the concept of merging his skills at web design, multimedia development and writing into a new form of storytelling media: Electronic Media Entertainment. His goal is to expand the universe of a story from being confined to one medium (a book, a game, a graphic novel) into a multi-layered universe that encompasses a variety of media types.

He currently lives in Owings Mills, Maryland and is a member of various clubs in the Baltimore Metropolitan area.

the apollyon game

The floor was littered with the debris of human bodies, wasted and butchered. At the center of this otherwise ordinary space was an object of simplicity, stained by streaks of crimson and entrails, looking deceptively innocent. It was a bowl, fashioned plainly, white in color and smooth to the touch. Inside was a shallow pool of some unidentified liquid, thick in consistency and corrosive in odor.

A small man in a yellow pastel suit casually walked through the aftermath, kicking pieces of flesh and trash from his path. He stopped at the bowl and peered down at it. His breaths became heavier with each passing moment until he finally knelt down and collected the bowl. With his index finger, he swirled the rim, collected a thin layer of material there, put his finger into his mouth and sucked on it passionately. His eyes closed as he savored the taste, but this was not the time to indulge. The bowl went into a plastic grocery bag. As he left the room, he noticed the decapitated head of a young boy—no more than sixteen—staring at him with a gaping mouth and widened eyes.

"Thank you, Joseph," the man spoke quietly. "Thank you for being you."

At the corner of Holmes Street and Drake Lane sat a single apartment building, off from the rest of the complex, built of brick and aged on the outside by decades of weather and neglect. The inside was renovated however, and the apartments themselves were spacious. On the top floor, in unit 3D, resided Mitchell Maclaroy, but tonight he wasn't home. Away on business, he left the place to be watched by his younger sister Portia, a rebellious girl with an affinity for being a darkly dressed outsider.

It was a little before eight and darkness had taken over the sky. Portia stood on the balcony and observed the night, breathing in damp air that had been chilled by a rain shower some hours earlier. The moon was a faint sliver on this night, its glow barely cutting through the blackness of the sky. This was certainly not a normal evening—Portia had already reconciled that—it was a night where strange energies lingered in the air. She could taste them on her tongue and feel them in her nostrils as she inhaled deeply, held her breath for a moment, and then exhaled slowly. This process was an ingesting and expelling of the night's energies, or so she hoped. They would be needed for what lay ahead.

Over the next quarter hour came a number of guests. Five arrived during this time: what a collection of diverse personalities Portia had gathered. She had invited them all over to play a game, a new game she had purchased over the internet through one of her social media groups. It required six to play, but Portia really considered herself having only two friends. Liz, an Asian-American gothic girl whose wardrobe was just as black as Portia's, and Kerry, a slender boy who had just recently burst out of the closet with an abundance of flamboyance that was ever evident in his decorative eye make-up and loud jewelry. The other three were people Portia had known but was not necessarily close to.

Latoya Russell was as "hood" as you could get. She was tall, naturally muscular and had a mouth and personality—and mouth—that would overshadow anyone else in the room if she felt like making her thoughts on anything known. Portia had met her in rehab last year, and the two had kept in touch since. That was their bond; beyond that, they had very little in common.

Callie Creedlove came from an entirely different world than either Portia or Latoya. She was fond of lacrosse, her Tuesday youth group after school and, unlike Latoya, rarely had anything negative to say about anyone. In grade school, Callie and Portia were the best of friends but by their teens their divergent interests and decidedly different family lives drove a wedge between them. Now, they would consider each other friends only by the loosest of definitions, so when Portia called Callie to come over for a small gathering, Callie was equally surprised and excited. She had longed to renew her friendship with Portia but had never been able to find a way to do it. Tonight could possibly provide that very opportunity.

Lastly was Meredith Mumpower, a neighbor of Portia's brother Mitchell who lived in the same apartment building. Portia had known her for a few weeks through her brother. Meredith cared for men, clothes and reality television. Not much else sparked her curiosity from what Portia could tell as the woman only seemed to engage in conversations about those three topics. She was friendly though, so Portia saw her as a good candidate for the sixth player in the game, a spot that she was having a hard time to fill.

"So, what's up with this game?" asked Latoya, already becoming bored with the company at the party.

"Yeah," Meredith chimed in. "What is this thing? I've never heard of it. What's it called again?"

"*Probitas Comburo*," Portia answered.

"Sounds like Latin or something. Where did you find this game?" Kerry asked, not wanting the conversation to go on without him.

"On the internet, where else? This guy I met at Otakon last year told me about it. It took him a while to track down someone who actually had the game pieces. Some guy in Germany was selling original copies online so I bought one."

"Must have been expensive," Meredith remarked.

Portia smiled at her, "More than you can imagine."

"And what is the purpose of this game? I mean, what kind of game is it?" Callie asked.

Portia now had the full attention of her guests. They had managed to form a semi-circle around her, focused on her every word. It wasn't often Portia was afforded such attention. She had generally been ignored in public life.

"It's kind of like a truth game, you know. Like truth or dare, but it's got a bit of a Halloweenish tone to it."

"This isn't like devil worship or something?" Callie asked, her voice showing great caution. "You know I'm not comfortable with anything like that."

Kerry groaned at her worrying. "God, really? I mean, I shouldn't have said *God* because that might offend you too. But I mean, come on. It's a freakin' game! You're not going to Hell if you play a game that has some twisted pictures on the cards so stop worrying."

He flipped his hand towards Callie in a dismissive manner. For her part, she didn't see reason to protest any further. Portia was staring at them both and for a moment Callie felt a rush of coldness from Portia's gaze. Perhaps she was imagining things because the scowl quickly turned into a grin.

"No, this isn't devil worshipping, Callie. But please don't thump the Bible at us tonight. Most of us aren't really up to hearing that here. It's a party, try to have fun."

Liz, who had been in the bedroom for most of the conversation, entered the room with a box full of items that ranged from bottles of alcohol to small closed containers whose contents would have to be guessed at.

"You got everything, right Liz?" Portia asked her friend.

Liz labored to get the box into the living room and sighed with relief when she no longer had to carry it. "Yeah, everything's here. I guess we can start this shit."

"Sounds good. Okay, let's play."

"This better be fun Portia. I ain't staying here all night for some bullshit," Latoya warned as she read through text messages on her cell phone.

"Trust me, Latoya. You won't be bored," Portia smiled.

The living room was the largest room in the apartment and came with the standard beige carpet and off-white walls. A sliding glass door the led to the balcony. A flat screen TV had been affixed to the wall; a video game system, sat on the floor beneath it. Aside from that, the room had no other real furniture. Portia had moved, a small loveseat into the dining room so everyone could sit in a circle and play the game.

She put the cards out first. They were elegantly designed with intricate spirals, circles and triangles that surrounded a symbol in the center. The symbol was of a closed eye that was either crying or bleeding between its lids. There were three stacks as Portia explained: the Spirit cards, the Time cards and the Challenge cards. A white bowl was placed at the very center of everyone, and Portia seemed to take great care in making sure it was precisely in the center of the circle. Finally, she set the oddest part of this game down: the Pith Dice. It was quite larger than any dice most in the party had ever seen, about the size of a two liter soda bottle. The dice was really one piece consisting of two pyramids, stacked end-to-end, with the same intricate patterns etched on each of its polished bronze sides. At the center of each of the six sides was a number which looked as if painted on by an unsteady but deliberate hand. The numbers went from one to seven, skipping the number three.

Latoya picked up the dice and turned it in her hands. "What the fuck is this? This shit's heavy."

"That's the Pith Dice," Liz explained, showing a growing irritation with Latoya's bluntness.

"A what?" Latoya asked, rolling the die back into the circle.

"Pith. Dice. P-p-pith," Liz repeated slowly.

Latoya noted the attitude, "Don't get smart, alright little chow mein. I will go off on you in her house, trust that."

"All right, all right, we're not here to have a fight," Kerry said, breaking up the fight before it got started. "So, Portia how do we play this thing?"

Portia was about the business of lighting candles. She set a few in the kitchen nearby, some in the bathroom and another two dozen in the living room with them. She then turned off the lights and joined the circle.

"Is that really necessary?" Callie complained. "I told you, I don't …"

"Yeah, yeah, blah blah church girl. We know," Kerry interrupted. "This is supposed to be a spooky game. You *have* to turn the lights off."

Portia took one of the candles in her hand to bring some more light into the circle. She proceeded to explain the rules of the game to the party.

One player, the *Soultender*, would take the Pith Dice and turn the top half clockwise according to the number on the bottom half, then turn the bottom half counterclockwise according to the number on the top. Once they were done, the Soultender would pick a partner, a *Soulcatcher*, for that round.

The Soulcatcher would have the choice of answering a question from the Soultender. If the Soulcatcher chose not to answer the Soultender's question, the Soultender would use the top number of the Pith Dice to draw a Challenge card (face down), the bottom number on the Pith Dice to draw a Spirit card (face down), and then draw the first Time card (face up).

At that point, the Soulcatcher would turn the Challenge card face up and would have to complete the task on the Challenge card within the time allotted on the Time card. Should the Soulcatcher not want to complete the challenge, they still have the option of answering the Soultender's question at any time to end the round.

If the Soulcatcher completes the task in the time allowed or answers the Soultender's question, they win that round, keep the Spirit card face down as part of their hand, and the game continues. If they do not, the Soultender shows the Spirit card drawn and the fate of the Soulcatcher is determined. If they lose a round, the Soulcatcher can choose to use a Spirit card in their hand, if they have any, to determine their fate in the game. A Spirit card can save a player from being removed from the game, require the round to start over again, or (most likely) remove the player from the game.

"Sounds complicated," Callie commented as she cautiously scanned over the game pieces before her.

"Not so much," Portia reassured.

There was an awkward silence as if no one wanted to instigate the game's beginning. Liz braved up to it and placed her hands on the Pith Dice. She marveled over its design, its intricately detailed swirls and lines, and with a hint of wonder in the pupils of her eyes, turned the top clockwise twice, which revealed the number five. She then turned the bottom counterclockwise five times, which revealed the number seven. Looking around the circle, she knew who she wanted to ask a question of first.

"Latoya," she grinned, "I choose you."

Latoya had not really been paying attention to what was going on for the last few minutes, preoccupied with text messaging. She awoke from her trance and stared deadly at Liz. She had no time for this girl, and her interest in the game was waning with each passing moment. However, she'd play, just to see what would happen—if the game itself was any fun at all.

"All right," Latoya scoffed. "Ask what you want."

Liz took satisfaction in finally starting the process. She gently placed the Pith Dice down on the carpet and folded her hands together, as if pondering some great question about the universe. What came out was less than transcendent.

"Do you hate white people?" she asked.

Latoya, who had been chewing gum rather obsessively, stopped her chewing immediately and threw an insulted look at the gothic girl across from her. Liz turned the Time Card over, revealing three minutes.

"I don't need three minutes to answer this. No, I don't hate white people. I mean, y'all get on my nerves sometimes with the crazy shit y'all do. I mean, look at you."

Liz sat up straight, offended at what she thought was about to be an assault on her person.

"What about me? I'm not even white!" she protested.

"I mean, you act white. All that mess you wear. Black eyeliner, black lipstick, black fingernail polish. What is that? You supposed to scare somebody with that?" Latoya asked.

"It's being original, not that someone like you would know anything about that. You're hip hop ghetto trash 101," Liz responded.

"Now, let's not get nasty with this. She answered the question, she gets the Spirit card," Portia interrupted, not wanting the game to get contentious so early.

Liz drew to the seventh Spirit card and slid it over to Latoya, face down. Latoya looked at the card, turned her face up in disgust at what she saw, and then sat it face down in front of her. It was now her turn however, and Latoya grabbed the Pith Dice and instantly began turning the top, and then the bottom, in a reckless manner.

"I'm gonna ask your boy over there a question," Latoya said, pointing at Kerry. "Have you ever slept with a girl?"

Without hesitating, Latoya turned over the Time card. It marked one minute. Kerry was clearly caught off guard by the question and stumbled over his words for a few seconds. He then opted defiantly to take the challenge instead. Latoya drew the fifth card in the Challenge deck and turned it over.

"You must consume half a bowl of a clear spirit before the time expires, or offer your fate to the *spirits*," read Callie, taking more of an interest in the game now.

"Spirits?" Latoya questioned.

"It means liquor," Kerry snapped. "Someone get the damn vodka before the time runs out."

Liz had it next to her in the box she brought from the other room. She poured the white bowl half full of Grey Goose and they all sat back and waited for Kerry to drink. He looked into the bowl and then the clock, seeing only thirty seconds left for him.

"That's a lot of vodka for one damn shot!" Kerry exclaimed, now realizing that a half bowl of vodka wasn't the easiest thing to drink down. "Can I just ..."

"Answer the question or drink the vodka," Portia cut in. "Or, leave your fate to the *spirits*."

There was something eerie in the way Portia spoke, but Kerry was willing to play along with this game. He grabbed the bowl and sloppily gulped down the drink. Halfway through, he coughed and stopped drinking. The room laughed and started to chide him.

"Come on, Kerry! All mouth and no game!" Liz smirked.

"You've got ten seconds to finish that," reminded Portia, the second hand on the clock in the living room ticking away without concern.

With a gasp, and a few more snide remarks from the rest of the party, Kerry choked down the rest of the vodka with two seconds to spare. He dropped the bowl and shook his head in an attempt to endure the sting of drinking so much vodka in such a short period of time. He coughed, his eyes watered, he snorted, but after a few moments finally composed himself.

"Are you okay?" Callie asked, patting him on the back.

Kerry pushed her hand away and coughed again before answering, "I'm fine. Give me the card girl!"

He smiled happily at Latoya, having bested her in this round, and Latoya drew his Spirit card. She nodded to him, impressed that he could actually drink that much and not vomit on the spot. It appeared that some of the intensity of this diverse group was, for the moment, lessened. Perhaps that was the point of the game to begin with, Latoya thought, as she looked over Kerry with new admiration.

"My turn," Kerry exclaimed as he coughed one more time before picking up the Pith Dice.

He turned the top and bottom and revealed a five for the top and a two for the bottom. The Time card had two minutes on its face. Kerry didn't know exactly who he wanted to ask a question of but decided, since it was her game, to go for Portia. She nodded and waited for Kerry—who seemed all too enamored with the attention of everyone in the circle—to ask his question. He looked up, then down, then stretched his arms out, all before finally getting to his query.

"What are you afraid of?" he asked.

Portia took a moment to look around at the circle. It was a question most there wanted her to answer, as most of them didn't think Portia was afraid of anything. She carried herself as an outcast—as a tough girl—and that perception went unchallenged until now. What could someone who showed such disdain for most of life's trappings have to be afraid of?

"Losing this game," she said flatly.

There was a groan from someone in the circle. Portia didn't catch who it was but had her suspicions. No one apparently believed her answer and Portia knew this, but she also knew she had in fact told the truth.

Without waiting for complaints, she motioned to Kerry to draw her Spirit card. He did so with an upturned lip and handed it to her. Portia looked over the card and smiled to herself as if she had just gotten away with robbery. She then picked up the Pith Dice and continued the game, drawing a one for the top number and a seven for the bottom. The Time card had ten seconds on it and she quickly looked to Callie as her *Soulcather*.

"Are you really a virgin?" Portia asked bluntly.

"Ooh, that's a good one!" Kerry chirped. "Now we're getting into the good stuff. Ms. Virgin Callie, a real virgin or not?"

"I don't think that's an appropriate question," Callie debated.

"You've got five more seconds," Portia said coldly.

"This isn't fun," Callie said, "I don't think I want to play this game anymore."

"Answer the question or you lose," said Portia.

"No," Callie spat.

Portia pushed a Spirit card to Callie who didn't seem interested in looking at it. Instead, she stood up and left the room. Portia watched her angrily as she headed to the bathroom, the card still sitting in her spot.

"Let's just keep playing. Let the little bitch cry," Liz said.

Portia hesitated and looked around the room as if expecting something to happen. After a moment, she twisted the Pith Dice again and drew the Time card. The time was five minutes. This time, Portia took a moment to pick her *Soulcatcher*. Meredith was her choice, and Portia knew exactly what she wanted to ask.

"You've been so quiet tonight," Portia muttered under her breath, almost in a whisper.

"Just watching," Meredith replied. "Wish your brother was here. This would be a bit more fun if he was."

"Really?" Portia spat at Meredith. "Funny you should mention him. Because I know you're not really all that quiet. In fact, you make a lot of noise when you're fucking don't you?"

Kerry and Liz looked at each other stunned while Latoya stopped her texting completely. Meredith bit her lip, wanting badly to rip into Portia but thought better of it.

"If you've been listening to me and your brother having sex, that's kind of creepy, you know. Maybe if you had a man, you'd find better things to do."

"It's not my brother I heard you having sex with."

"Aw, shit!" Latoya shouted. "Gettin' real now!"

Meredith started to fidget where she sat. The truth behind the claim was evident in her demeanor so there was no use denying it. Portia continued to stare at Meredith, her anger and bitterness at this woman's betrayal of her brother so palpable now that Meredith swore she saw fire in Portia's eyes.

"So my question is, who was it?" Portia asked.

The clock on the wall shook on its own. Liz was the only one who noticed it, but thought it to be a coincidence. Not wanting to go any further with this, Meredith elected to take the Challenge instead of letting her personal business be spilled out in a room full of strangers. The Challenge card asked for a dead bug to be placed in the bowl and consumed.

"What kind of shit is that?" Latoya asked. "This is getting stupid, Portia. I mean, she ain't eating no damn bug. Where are you going to find one anyway?"

"I've got one," said Liz as she went to the box of items and pulled out a jar.

Inside the jar was a dead roach. She quickly dumped its lifeless body into the white bowl and pushed the container over to Meredith.

"You've got four minutes left," Portia said.

"Fuck this, I'm out of here. Go fuck yourself, bitch."

"You would know about fucking, wouldn't you? But don't worry, my brother doesn't know. I didn't tell him. I hoped you would."

Meredith stood up and headed to the door. She stopped, not wanting to let this go just yet. She turned back to Portia, seething now with anger, and pointed her finger at her lover's sister.

"You don't know shit about me, okay! It's none of your business what happens between me and your brother."

"You can't leave," Portia said, ignoring Meredith's words. "You have to finish the game."

"I'm not finishing this crap! You know what you can do with your little game."

"Time's up," Liz said, looking at the clock.

"Turn the card over," Portia demanded.

Meredith scoffed and continued to the door. Portia stomped over to the deck and drew the Spirit card. She turned it over and walked over to Meredith, who was at the front door now, and showed it to her. Out of pure interest, Meredith looked at the card. It had a demonic female figure on it, clad in red clothes with grey skin and fire pouring from between her legs. The top of the card had the title *Mellachious* and below the drawing was an inscription which Meredith read aloud.

"The Spirit you've called is Mellachious, the demon of lust and pain. You have lost this round *Soulcatcher*, and are now owned by Mellachious. Your judgment has been told." Meredith laughed at the card and threw it to the ground. "I guess I can leave now. I'm out of the game, right?"

Portia didn't say anything. She seemed to be waiting for something. Meredith just stared back, and when Portia didn't have more words for her, she turned towards the door to leave.

Without warning, Meredith was flung backwards to the wall, pinned against it by some unseen force. She let out a shriek and then coughed as blood spilled from her mouth. Kerry, Liz and Latoya ran into the foyer to see what was going on. Callie emerged from the bathroom, streaks of dried tears on her face, and immediately went to help Meredith.

"What the fuck? What the fuck?" screamed Latoya.

Callie turned to Portia who seemed to be enjoying whatever was going on. Meredith's arms began to twist on themselves, her knees bending inwards with a sickening series of cracks and pops. Callie and Kerry were now both trying to pull Meredith from the wall, but their efforts stopped when another set of hands reached from within the wall and took hold of Meredith's midsection. They were sickly hands, reddish brown with green sores covering the flesh. Callie and Kerry backed away and could only watch as Meredith gargled up bubbles of blood. More hands clawed at her from within the wall and, with a sudden thrust, pulled parts of her body into the wall while leaving others to burst throughout the room in a shower of tissue and blood. Kerry and Latoya screamed while Liz turned to Portia in amazement. Portia wiped the blood from her mouth slowly, savoring the moment with a look of satisfaction.

"That was for my brother," Portia exclaimed.

"What the fuck was that?" Latoya screamed. "This is some sick shit."

"That's the game, I told you the rules," Portia said.

"You did this!" Latoya yelled again, now face to face with Portia. "I don't know what kind of sick devil worshipping shit this is but I'm out of here. You're a sick little bitch, Portia."

Stone faced, Portia dismissed Latoya's rants and walked back to the living room. Kerry stood stunned for a moment, but soon followed Latoya's lead and headed towards the front door. Portia gave them the same warning she gave Meredith, but they weren't having any of it. They opened the front door of the apartment and headed into the hallway. Callie took one more look at Portia who was about the business of turning the Pith Dice again. She wondered if the game would continue even if they weren't in the circle. If so, Portia could choose whoever she wanted: if that person didn't complete the task or answer her question, they'd suffer the same fate as Meredith. It did make Callie questioned why she hadn't been attacked when her Spirit card was drawn, but there was no time to ponder.

Another problem quickly put those worries to rest. As Callie tried to leave behind Kerry and Latoya, she noticed they hadn't gotten too far into the hallway. She looked over Kerry's shoulder to see what had stopped them.

"I don't believe this," Kerry whispered to Callie. "I think we have to stay."

Standing between them and the staircase that led downstairs was a grotesquely obese man holding a meat cleaver. His head was bald and covered in spots that also dotted his shoulders and arms beneath a white cotton undershirt that was two sizes too small. The shirt itself was covered in a variety of colored stains that one could only speculate the origins of. He stroked the cleaver against his stomach which billowed out of the bottom of his undershirt. He seemed to enjoy scratching the sharpened end against a rash of bleeding bumps around his bellybutton. He made no attempt to speak, but grunted and wheezed at the trio. It was clear that he had no intention of moving from that spot, and none of them wanted to get within arm's reach of him and that cleaver.

"Get back inside! Get back inside!" Latoya ordered the others as she pushed backwards into the apartment.

She closed the door and locked it behind her. Kerry and Callie walked back to the living room—Callie looking for another way out of the apartment and Kerry to confront Portia.

"Okay, I'm on your side, you know. We're friends," he said to Portia, almost pleading with her. "I mean, I know you're into some weird shit, obviously, and it was fun and cute and all but … really? This is some twisted shit, a bit much for me, and I … I … I think I just want to go home. Okay?"

"Sit the fuck down," Portia demanded.

Kerry's pleading stopped as he backed up. Portia and Liz both stared him down, as if daring him to continue his whining. Callie came back into the living room after looking in all the other rooms for an exit.

"There's no fire escape or anything. We're too high to jump off the balcony: we'd break our necks. So, that's why you wanted us to play here," Callie said directly to Portia.

"Smart, isn't she?" Portia laughed. "You should sit down too. We've still got a ways to go."

"I'm not playing anymore, remember," Callie countered.

"I don't think we have a choice," Kerry whimpered, already back at his seated position in the circle.

"Latoya!" Portia yelled. "Come sit down."

Latoya was at the front door, feverishly trying to send out text messages and becoming increasingly frustrated that they weren't going through.

"That's not going to work," Portia told her. "You can keep trying but the phone is not sending out anything until we're done."

"How the fuck do you know that?" Latoya yelled. "Someone's going to get this message. And when I tell my brothers what you did, they're going to …"

"They're not going to do anything because they won't know anything because you won't tell them anything," Portia said in a controlled and even tone. "Now, put the phone away and sit down. We have to keep playing and I'm picking you as my next Soulcatcher."

"The hell you are!" Latoya said and rushed at Portia.

The two girls wrestled to the floor. Latoya swung violently at Portia who covered up. Liz tried to pull Latoya off but did not have the strength to control her. Kerry noticed the Time card had already been turned over. It revealed a minute and a half for this next question, but Portia had yet to ask it. She was desperately trying to between punches and kicks from Latoya.

Liz finally managed to wrestle Latoya backwards, wrapping her arms around her neck and her legs around her waist to force some separation between the two fighting girls. Portia stood up and put her hand to her face which was now scratched and bleeding. She spit at Latoya and pushed her black hair out of her eyes before finally asking her next question.

"Latoya! Do you think you're for real?"

Once her anger subsided, Latoya stopped fighting against Liz's restraint and asked to be let up. Liz complied, untangling their bodies. Callie and Kerry watched with anticipation, expecting Latoya to strike Portia at any second. Instead, she picked up her cell phone and tried to make a call. The battery had died. Seeing this, Latoya laughed at the phone and then threw it at Portia as hard as she could.

"Fuck you," is all Latoya could muster.

"Uh, you better answer her or do the challenge or something," Kerry warned. "Who knows what the hell is going to happen if you don't."

A loud slam came from the master bedroom. Latoya turned to look into the bedroom but didn't dare get any closer. She looked next at the clock, seeing only thirty seconds left for her time. Panic began to set in. There wasn't anything she could do but answer the question or take the challenge.

"Before you say anything," Portia started, "you should know that if you lie it's the same as failing the challenge or not answering. They'll know if you lie."

"*They'll* know?" Callie asked. "Who will know?"

She didn't get an answer as Portia had her entire focus on Latoya. Latoya's focus was on the splattered body parts in the foyer. That would be her if she didn't answer honestly. It was a simple question though.

"I am," she said.

"You lied." Portia responded.

"How are you going to tell me whether or not I'm for real? Do you believe this bitch?"

Portia snickered to herself and sat back down in the circle, lighting another candle as some had been blown out during all the commotion earlier.

"When we were little kids Latoya, you were just as much of an outsider as I was. Your brothers called you weird, your mother called you weird, everyone called you weird. You used to like the same shit I did. We used to read the same occult books, go into the woods and pretend we were summoning spirits and all that stuff."

"That was a long time ago," Latoya said in a much calmer tone.

"Yeah, but all of a sudden you tried to act like you were 'hood' when you've never set foot inside a ghetto. You started wearing this shit you've got on, talking like you're on *BET* and hanging out with a bunch of assholes. Assholes who, by the way, beat the shit out of me in eighth grade."

"So that's what this shit is all about? You mad because my girls beat you down. I told them not to. I told them …"

"You didn't stand up for me. You didn't do anything. You're phony as shit, Latoya. You know that and so do I."

"So what?"

"So, you lied, and that means you lost."

The time had expired. Latoya couldn't look at Portia any longer. It was clear that Portia wanted Latoya to come to some admission of guilt for being phony, or for abandoning their friendship in order to be more socially accepted. Latoya didn't care. There was no great revelation. There was no agreement. Instead, there was just resentment that she had been tricked into this trap and couldn't get out. Whether or not she felt she was a fraud in personality, Portia's deception nullified any remorse or repentance she could possibly feel. Now, she just waited for the final card to turn over.

"Look at it," Portia said, holding the Spirit card in her outstretched hand.

Latoya had turned her back to Portia completely and didn't care to read what was on the Spirit card. She remembered the rules of the game though, and it was possible that the Spirit card was not murderous, but perhaps forgiving. The one she had collected earlier was certainly not. It held a mischievous demon whose name she couldn't recall at the moment. That creature would certainly lead to a horrific death.

Taking her chances, Latoya turned back to Portia and took the card. She sighed for a moment and then looked at its face. Her fortunes were no better with this one. It was a spirit whose name she also couldn't pronounce, but the illustration told the whole story. The image was of a three-mouthed creature with a singular eye, devouring victims at will. She sat down and closed her eyes, waiting for the end.

"Come on with it then!" she shouted. "Let's get this over with!"

Nothing happened. After a few seconds, everyone began to look around wondering if something was going to happen. Perhaps the spirits were no longer interested. Perhaps a rule had been overlooked. Perhaps Latoya had answered correctly after all.

Portia was not pleased but Latoya couldn't have been happier.

"Seems *they* know better," she exclaimed, rising to her feet now. "Your bullshit is broke, Portia. And I don't give a shit if that fat bastard is sitting outside. I'm getting out of here. You can finish your game on your own."

Feeling vindicated, Latoya picked her phone up from the floor. The battery apparently had regained its charge. She smirked to herself and then dialed her brother's phone number. A ring! She put the phone to her ear, eagerly waiting for her brother to answer.

A sharp pain quickly shot through her skull. She dropped the phone and put her hand to her ear. It fell off into her hand. She held it in her palm, bleeding heavily from the side of her head. Another crash came from the bedroom, same as before, and this time Latoya could see what had made the sound. The three-mouthed demon, very real and larger than she had estimated from the card's illustration, sat in the doorway to the master bedroom. She collapsed to the ground, the pain now shooting from both sides of her head as her other ear fell to the carpet.

Callie and Kerry screamed again, seeing the blood filling the carpet and Latoya grasping at her face. Her nose slid down past her lips, leaving a trail of blood and mucus. Latoya quivered as her body continued to fall to pieces, and just before she passed out from the pain, the demon snatched what remained of her body, dragged it into the bedroom, and slammed the door shut. The sounds of eating—ravenous chomping and slurping—came from the room for a minute or so. Then, all was silent again, and Portia went back to the Pith Dice.

"Enough!" Kerry yelled. "This is insane Portia! Stop this now! Why are you doing this?"

"Oh dear, he wants a motive," Portia grinned to Liz.

Liz was about the business of washing the white bowl in the sink. She tossed the roach down the drain and wiped the bowl dry before returning to the living room.

"You all are jerks, that's the motive," Liz explained.

Portia looked at the bowl as Liz sat it back in the middle of the circle. She became preoccupied with it as she continued to talk to what remained of the party.

"You see, there's no justice in this world. People like Latoya, who was as fake as you can get, just go on hurting people and no one does anything. Meredith can betray my brother and I'm just supposed to live with it. Not anymore."

"What did I do to you Portia? Huh?" Kerry asked. He wasn't scared anymore, as it was likely he would be meeting his end soon if this continued.

"You? You're just as fake as the rest of them. But we'll get to that later, won't we. Oh, I do have questions for you my friend."

Liz decided to add to the story. "And Callie," she started, "everything about you is fake. The bible thumping, the Ms. Average Good Girl routine. We know you have secrets. Portia's told me. You two used to be friends and you turned your back on her just like Latoya. All of you screwed her over because you thought you could. Because she's not like you, because she's different."

"Yes, *all* of you did," Portia said coldly, turning the ends of the Pith Dice as she did.

The emphasis on *all* did not escape Liz. Portia had just as cold a stare for her as she did for the rest of the party. Bewildered at why her friend had turned on her, Liz started to protest being the next Soulcatcher but Portia would hear none of it. Kerry and Callie had no remorse for her and simply sat and watched.

"I know you are the one who told my mother I was using. That's how I get sent to that shit hole I met Latoya in. Don't bother denying it, I know it was you. So my question is, friend: why did you do it? Was it out of concern for me?"

Looking at the Time card and seeing she had only forty-five seconds to answer, Liz didn't hesitate.

"Yes, I was concerned for you Portia. That's why I did it. You know I'm your friend. We're just alike."

"We're nothing alike, Liz. What, because we wear the same clothes you think you're like me? You're some goth girl. I never claimed to be that."

"Doesn't matter. It's my turn though. So hand me …"

"Wait, wait, wait," Portia stopped her. "How do I know that's the truth? Let's wait to see the time run out."

"Of course it's the truth. What, do you think I'm lying to you?"

"No, not to me," Portia answered. "I think you're lying to yourself. You didn't give a rat's ass about me being healthy. You did it because we had a fight about Justin."

"Really? You think I ratted you out because of Justin?"

"Well, time will tell now won't it?"

The second hand on the clock continued to tick. Five seconds were left and Liz began to sweat. She wondered if in her mind she had convinced herself that she ratted Portia out because of concern, but in her heart it was from jealousy. As the second hand reached its final tick, she realized what the truth actually was.

"Oh no," Liz whispered.

Portia turned the Spirit card over. It was the Jackyl, perhaps the most devious of all the Spirits in the deck.

Liz looked around the room, terrified that something would happen. She stood up and stumbled over one of the lit candles, knocking it to the carpet. She stomped out the flame and then sought somewhere safe to stand. She didn't want to be near the bedroom, or the front door, or the kitchen with all the ways she could be murdered in there. The only place she thought would be safe was next to Portia.

"Please, please Portia," Liz cried, grabbing at the Soultender's shoulders. "Make it stop. Don't let it happen. You can stop it! It says so in the game book. You can end this if you want to."

Callie and Kerry took note of this. Callie immediately went to Liz's box to look for the book. Portia and Liz continued arguing, which was becoming so intense the two girls had lost all concern for the game and knocked over the bowl and the stack of Challenge cards. Kerry looked at the scattered deck, paused for a moment, and then began the task of putting them back into a stack.

Amidst all the confusion, a nasally snicker was repeating itself, growing louder and more insane with each iteration. The group soon noticed the sound, and Liz immediately began crying, trying to use Portia as a shield. She grabbed her friend by the arms so if anything would do harm to her, it would do harm to Portia as well.

The strategy didn't work. Liz felt cold, rough hands at her shoulders and claws digging into the top of her chest. The snickering was now at her ear, and she knew what it was that had her. Portia freed herself from Liz's grasp and stepped back, watching the Jackyl as it caressed its prey.

"Please. No," Liz muttered in a desperate cry.

The sobs only seemed to excite the Jackyl more, as it sniveled and snickered uncontrollably. It began humming as it danced its sharpened nails up and down the nape of Liz's neck. Its face was bright red with tattooed black lines and circles around its mouth, eyes and nose. While it tormented Liz, it wore a needle-toothed smile in a mouth twice the size of normal proportions to the rest of its head. The demon's reptilian eyes blinked twice, and the humming stopped. It remained as stiff as a board, still clasping its hands around Liz's upper body. She whimpered, waiting for the creature to make a move. It didn't. The Jackyl simply froze for a while, Liz still shaking in its demented embrace.

She thought to move. Maybe she could get away. Perhaps the thing was petrified, or something had gone wrong. This was her chance, if there was going to be one, and she took it.

Before she could take that first step, the Jackyl let loose an earsplitting howl and began ripping at Liz's flesh, tearing her into ribbons with each ravenous gashes. It cooed and giggled as Liz collapsed on the floor in a heap of her own tissue.

As her sobs waned the Jackyl looked over her and pretended to be saddened, stroking her body with the knuckles of its hand. Dabbling in some of her blood, it placed its finger in its mouth, tasting the juices it had collected. The demon looked to Callie, licked its hand clean of blood, and then began snickering again before disappearing into the shadows of the living room.

Portia returned to her seat in the circle and picked up the Pith Dice. Her next target was clear as she eyed Kerry with each turn of the object. In contrast, Kerry did everything he could to look away from Portia, not wanting to make eye contact with her. His body was shaking even though he tried desperately to control it.

"Fifty seconds," Portia remarked as she looked at the Time card. "Looks like enough time for you to try your hand."

"Just get this over with," Kerry replied bitterly.

Portia smiled at his defiance. Callie watched Kerry intently as he waited for Portia's question, and she couldn't help but notice beneath the shaking in Kerry's body a sense of impatience, as if he wanted to g.

"Are you really gay?" Portia asked her Soulcatcher.

Kerry went to the Challenge card and turned it over. His task was rather mundane: to fill the bowl with water and drink it. He did so eagerly, and in about fifteen seconds was done with his challenge.

Something was wrong, and Portia knew it. The look on her face was a mixture of surprise and disdain. Regardless, Kerry had won the round and thus won the right to roll the Pith Dice himself.

"Now it's my turn bitch!" he said with a glimmer of revenge in his voice.

"I'm not afraid," Portia said, "it's my game and I know the rules."

"Whatever, I'm ending this bullshit right now."

The door to the apartment shook with a large bang. All three players stood up immediately, their attention to the door and the heavy thuds that were being levied against it. Someone was knocking and would not be satisfied until the door was either opened or they knocked it down.

"You answer it. You're the host," Kerry said to Portia.

She scoffed at him and confidently walked to the door and without hesitating opened it. There stood the fat man from the hallway, breathing heavily, still brandishing his bloodied cleaver.

"Cheater!" he bellowed.

The words were enough for Portia to know what had happened. She looked back at Kerry and pointed to him. Callie also knew what had happened and turned to Kerry.

"You cheated?" she asked.

"Not necessarily. I reshuffled the deck when it got knocked over."

"That's it?"

"Yes. Well, no. I may have looked for an easy Challenge card and put it at the top."

"That would be cheating, Kerry."

"I know."

"Cheater! Cheater! Cheater!" the fat man continued.

He didn't wait for any invitation from Portia. The butcher pushed his girth past her on a straight course for Kerry. Not wanting to see what the punishment for cheating this kind of game was, Kerry ran into the kitchen to put something between him and the fat butcher. It wouldn't do him much good as the butcher smashed into the waist-high countertop that separated the living room from the kitchen, swiping at Kerry with his cleaver. The third swipe came close enough to Kerry's mouth that he could taste the metal of the blade on his lips.

With a terrified screech, Kerry jumped over the counter and ran towards the door. The butcher wasn't far behind and quickened his floor-shaking pursuit, repeating the word *cheater* as he went. Portia was knocked over by Kerry as he sprinted past her, out the front door, down the stairwell, screaming for help as he went. She smartly moved out of the way of the butcher who was still swinging his cleaver wildly as he followed Kerry.

Two were now left. Portia and Callie watched each other to see who would move first. Portia was concerned that Callie would try to escape as Kerry had, but the young blonde did not move from the living room. She simply waited for something to happen. Her mind told her to make for an escape, but who knows what other barriers—demonic or otherwise—the game would throw at her to keep her from leaving.

"We don't have to finish this, Portia. You've made your point."

Portia took offense to Callie's words. "My point? You don't know what my point is! This is not about making a point, this is about justice."

"How is this justice? You've murdered your friends."

"Give me a break, Callie. Friends? You think those people are my *friends*? You think you are my friend? You're dumber than I thought you were."

There was a muffled grunting coming from the open front door of the apartment. Callie could see a large shadow moving up the stairwell outside the apartment. As it moved towards the door, she gasped as she saw it was the Butcher returning with what remained of Kerry.

The body was barely held together by bones and threads of flesh, but the meat had been hacked all over. Kerry's arms, legs, torso and neck all bore deep slices that spilled red. Surprisingly, Kerry was still alive. His head was barely hanging on to the rest of his body, but his eyes moved back and forth beneath ever-closing eyelids. He was trying to speak, but the butcher's hand covered his mouth.

The fat man threw Kerry's body to the ground in the foyer and pointed at it. His shirt was afresh with new stains from Kerry's bodily fluids as he wiped sweat from his brow and mouth.

"Cheater," the butcher exclaimed one last time.

Kerry turned his eyes up to Callie. His head was twisted at an angle that was only possible because his neck was sliced halfway through. There was such sadness there. She wondered what prayers or deals he was making in his mind to the spirit world. There was something going on in his head, some moment of reckoning that in these last few seconds, she hoped he resolved.

A second later, the butcher raised his cleaver above his head and brought the sharp edge down with such force it split Kerry's skull in two. The contents of his head spilled onto the carpet, brains and blood and other liquids spurting from some places and bubbling in others.

Callie couldn't look, but Portia did, with a breath of satisfaction. The butcher quietly left through the front door, and in an unsettling gesture of civility, closed the door gently behind him.

Only two were left.

Callie was so frightened at what would come next she could feel the bile in her throat almost choke her. Her stomach was turning over itself. Her palms were glistening with perspiration. She had to do something before she was the next and final victim of Portia's twisted game.

"Why him?" she asked quietly.

"Like I said, he was a phony. Kerry and I slept together, regularly, but he kept acting like he was a queer. I have no idea why. Maybe because it's *en vogue* now, who knows. All I know is that he treated me like some dirty secret. It was disrespectful and he deserved to pay for it. You all do."

"What did I do to you, Portia? Huh? What am I so guilty of that you're going to throw me into this meat grinder you've thought up?"

Portia laughed, "I didn't think this up. This game has been around for centuries. It's made for the victimized to get justice."

Callie watched as Portia reached for the Pith dice. There wouldn't be much more time. She had to keep Portia talking while she simultaneously thought of a way out of this.

"It sounds more like a petty way to scream at the world," Callie uttered under her breath.

Portia heard the comment, and it enraged her enough to want to defend herself. She put the Pith Dice down for the moment. She needed to set Callie straight before the game ended.

"Listen to me," Portia shouted as she came face to face with Callie, "this isn't about me wanting to scream at the world. This isn't about revenge, even. It's about doing something right. There are too many of you phony people in the world—the uncreative, the unimaginative, and worst of all people like you, yeah, the self-righteous."

"I'm self-righteous?" Callie sarcastically replied. Portia missed the implication.

"Of course you are! All you religious people are. That's why you're the worst, and the last, in this game. You abandoned me when you 'found Jesus' and couldn't spend time with your friend of fifteen years because I was a bad influence. Isn't that right?"

"Portia, I—"

"No! Isn't that right?"

"Maybe," Callie confessed, throwing her hands up in admission. "Yeah, maybe you cutting yourself, getting high every single day, having sex with anyone who would pay attention to you … yes, maybe that didn't mesh well with my beliefs."

"Aren't you supposed to try and save me?"

"I knew better than to do that."

Portia scoffed. She turned back to the circle and went for the Pith Dice again. Callie still needed more time.

"Would you have listened? Or would you have just dismissed me?" she asked.

Portia picked up the dice but turned back to Callie to answer.

"Probably not. I don't have much use for religion."

"So either way, I would be doing wrong in your eyes. No matter what, you would have dismissed whatever I had to offer you because you have already predetermined my beliefs as being crap."

"Not your beliefs, just the organization that goes along with it. All those judgmental, tight-assed, middle America jackasses."

"And what you just said isn't judgmental? What you've done tonight isn't passing judgment on people?"

"People like me aren't the oppressors! Don't you get that Ms. Perfect? People like me aren't abusing little children. People like me aren't damning anyone who doesn't fit in our little box to Hell."

"So, you think anarchy and violence and spitefulness are better than even considering anything someone like me has to say?"

Callie's words were penetrating somewhat, but Portia had come too far. The voice in Portia's mind reminded her of how just her cause was. Callie was one of *them*, the type that she despised with everything in her being. The family life, the house, and the so-called values they had. It was everything she found offensive and oppressive. This, right here, tonight, was her liberation from that. It was her chance to spit in the face of that very concept, and she wasn't going to let any doubt prevent that from happening.

"Better to reign in Hell than serve in Heaven, right?" she smirked.

She spun the dice and proceeded to pick the Time card. It was a long session; two minutes. Seeing that her time was up, Callie calmly returned to the circle and sat down. After watching this game play out, she knew Portia was going to ask her something she either wouldn't answer or would be tricked into answering wrong. She had to answer correctly, no matter what. The Challenges and the Spirits were things she surely wanted to avoid at any cost.

With a deep breath, Portia asked her question. "If you're a believer, do you really think all that crap they say to you on Sundays is true? Do you think your God is going to save you tonight?"

The clock was ticking. Even though an answer sprung to her mind immediately, she didn't want to say it. This was a time to think, a time to learn from what the others had done wrong, which led to them having their body parts strewn about the room she sat in now.

Oh, that smell! The detritus in the room from all of Portia's victims was beginning to sicken Callie. It was becoming a distraction in her mind. The more she thought, the more intense the odor got. It was to the point that she believed it was penetrating her skin, crawling underneath her flesh and sticking to her insides.

No! Concentrate!

"What's taking so long?" Portia shouted. "Come on! Answer the question, Callie! You know the truth."

Callie just sat in the circle, her head down and her hands clasped in prayer. Of all things for her to do, this was the funniest to Portia. She stood up and hovered over Callie like a hawk over its prey.

"That's right, pray bitch! There's nothing there! There's no one to pray to! There's no one who is going to save your life, your ass, your soul tonight! God is a damned joke, and if *He* ever existed, He's long since died. Even if He did exist, as your pathetic people think, do you honestly think He could give a rat's ass that you play lacrosse and have perfect attendance at church and live in a nice house?"

Undaunted, Callie continued to sit. Ironically, she wasn't praying, she was deep in thought. The smells of the room, the visions of what she had seen tonight and Portia's ongoing tirade all were working against her. She wanted to answer cleanly. If she thought God was going to save her—and truly believed that in her soul—she wanted to say so. If there was doubt, she wanted to express that. In a sense, her waking mind would have to give way to her immanent consciousness for any kind of salvation.

"Callie!" Portia screamed.

Callie did not answer.

"You've got ten seconds! You had better answer!"

There was still time for thought. Not yet.

"Five seconds."

What was the answer?

"Four!"

Ah, yes, of course!

"Thr—"

"I do," Callie said flatly. "I do believe God will save me."

She covered her face as a tear trickled down her cheek. She had been honest, perhaps more honest than she had ever been in her entire life. Such honestly had exhausted her emotionally, and she continued to weep. Portia watched her for a moment, curious about what she was seeing. Anticipating the Spirits to claim their prize, Portia waited for a sound, a movement, a shifting shadow. None came.

Callie had answered truthfully.

Before Portia could protest, Callie had taken hold of the Spirit card she had not used earlier in the night. She didn't care what was on the card and left it face down in front of her. She did care to turn the Pith Dice and hope to turn Portia's own game against her.

The game piece had other plans. It spirited from Callie's hand and rested at the dead center of the circle next to the white bowl, as if the bowl had ripped it from her hands. She took a moment to observe it and then reached out to grab it again. Perhaps she was wrong. Perhaps the Spirits were coming to take her. A trace of fear crept into Callie's heart. She had answered honestly and she knew it. Was this game rigged that much?

During all this, the Spirit card Callie had received earlier in the game was turned face-side up. She looked down at it; seeing what was there gave her pause. Portia drew near her and looked at the card too. Both girls became entranced at what they saw, one out of relief and the other out of dread.

You have drawn the Angelic Savior, a spirit that will protect you should you have need. You may proceed to the next round as Soulcatcher, but your Soultender has lost and must suffer all the spirits drawn before.

The words sat heavy on the card with a painted image of an Indian woman dressed in blue robes with white clouds surrounding her arms and feet. It wasn't the image Callie had anticipated, but what else had been on on this evening?

For Portia, it was the ultimate defeat. She knew what the *Angelic Savior* was. It was one of very few cards in the deck that saved the Soulcatcher, and in particular, turning the full wrath of the game's demons on the Soultender.

"I don't believe it! No! No! No!" Portia screamed.

It was the card Callie had the entire time: the irony of this did not escape her. Despite all that had happened, it appeared she was indeed protected the entire time. Whether through divine intervention (as Callie suspected) or dumb luck (as Portia believed), this was the fate of the game. Portia's vengeance had been turned on her.

"You little bitch!" she yelled at Callie.

There was no time for argument. The air in the room turned numbingly cold. Both girls could see their breaths in the air. A light came from the Pith Dice, deep red and pulsating. The entire apartment was bathed in the unnatural glow which cast solid black shadows where it could not illuminate.

Then the laughing began. The Jackyl was lurking behind Portia, licking at its long nails while salivating over its lips. The fat butcher had also returned, appearing silently from behind Callie but paying her no attention at all. Whatever abomination had consumed Latoya earlier could be heard pounding at the walls of the bedroom, sounding as if it was starving for new flesh. Above Portia, the hands of the demon that had claimed Meredith swiped from beneath the surface, its talons curled into great hooks that nipped at the top of Portia's dark hair.

Even though she knew they were not there for her, Callie felt a great unease at their presence. She backed into the kitchen, the only place in the apartment where the red light was not so heavy, and folded her arms around herself.

"Help me," Portia whispered to Callie. "You have to help me."

Callie didn't know what to say. The demons were making their way towards Portia, slowly stalking her and savoring their victim's whimpers and sobs. She wanted to help Portia. Her mind was working ways in which she could. But there was nothing she could do. The power of whatever evil lay within this game was in full control. Portia had sealed her fate long before this moment, and nothing would be able to stop what was coming.

The Jackyl struck first, sinking its teeth deep into Portia's arm. It uncontrollably giggled and slurped as it tasted her blood on its tongue. The fat butcher was next, wrapping his massive hands around Portia's leg, tugging at her violently. The wall to Portia's left burst open and a long strand of greenish-brown flesh, dotted with boils and quivering bumps wrapped itself around her torso. Callie couldn't see what monster was at the other end, nor did she dare move from her spot to look. Lastly, the swiping talons from above Portia finally took hold of the top of her skull, the fingernails pressing deep into her head.

During this entire trauma, Portia had not let loose a single scream or cry. In fact, Callie could swear she saw a smile on Portia's face. Even as the blood flowed from her many wounds, the tendons in her legs stretched to snapping, her ribs cracking to the point of becoming powder and her skull compressing her brain, Portia stood silent with a smirk.

"Portia," Callie muttered, tears coming to her eyes as she watched her once-friend being mutilated before her eyes. "I'm sorry. I will pray for your soul."

The smirk turned into a scowl, and Portia spat blood at Callie just as the Jackyl took another bite of her. She then cocked her head to the side and bit her lip, drawing more blood on her own, and licked the fresh wound clean with her tongue.

"Keep your prayers bitch. The Devil is my messiah!"

A second later, her body was ripped into pieces. Callie let out a cry but it was too late. Her vision was blinded by the red glare of the Pith Dice, which had grown so intense that she needed to cover her eyes with her palms for fear they'd be burned out of her skull. A sickening noise of eating and laughing whirled throughout the room like a foul wind. After a few seconds, it dispersed, as did the light.

Callie opened her eyes slowly and slid her palms from her face. The room was empty now. Neither the demons nor any remains of Portia had been left behind. The litter of the other victims still about the room, scattered here and there, rotting and festering.

In that moment, Callie's sympathy for Portia had vanished. There was nothing to be remorseful about. Portia was not her responsibility, and whatever evil she had conjured had lay claim to her soul long before tonight. The only thing Callie had done was save herself from becoming another victim.

She went to the center of the living room where the Pith Dice and the white bowl still remained. Both were stained with the waste of murder. Inside the bowl were pieces of all the victims. She could see a slab of flesh with a tattoo that she recognized from Kerry, a finger that belonged to Meredith, several teeth—one of which was gold plated—that belonged to Latoya, and a clump of hair that was clearly Liz's. Nothing in the bowl that she could see was of Portia and Callie knew why.

She remembered that earlier Liz had said Portia could stop the game if she wanted to. Perhaps Portia had done so with her final words.

As Callie had been embraced by her God, so too had Portia.

The front door of the apartment swung open. Callie turned to see who or what had forced its way into inside. She hoped it was the police. Surely someone had heard the noise and screams during the night. How she would explain being the only living person at a scene of such dismemberment was of great concern.

Instead, a small man wearing a yellow pastel suit walked through the open door. He casually observed the aftermath in the apartment as he walked to the white bowl on the floor. Callie watched him as he passed by, paying her no attention at all.

He picked up the bowl, swirled the inside of the blood-stained porcelain with his index finger and then sucked on the residue he had gathered. A grin crossed his lips and as he placed the bowl inside a plastic grocery bag and tied it shut.

"Who are you?" Callie said.

The man did not answer.

"Did you hear me? I said, 'Who are you?' What are you doing?"

Still ignoring her, he proceeded towards the open door. Callie followed him for a moment, but then stopped as the smell of the dead overwhelmed her again. She clutched at her stomach but regained her composure.

"Don't you have anything to say?" she pleaded, feeling sick and saddened as she realized fully what had happened tonight.

The man in the yellow suit stopped. He scratched the back of his head and turned to look at Callie. She could see him clearly now. His ears were large, his eyes a light blue, his teeth as yellow as his suit and his head balding.

"Thank you for being you, Callie," the man said.

With that, he continued out the front door. Callie followed him into the stairwell and watched him, puzzled and shaken, as he walked out of the apartment building into the blackness of the night.

luna stone

Luna Stone was born in Pittsburgh Pennsylvania on January 22nd 1997. She lives with her mother and step-father in her small home town while attending highschool. She enjoys writing, drawing, painting, photography, and reading. Her first goal was met after she was published in The Immanent World. That goal was to be published in a book before graduating high school. Now her goal is to write poems and stories that encourage the young and old to accept one another and be true to themselves.

a million and one

A million miles I've traveled.
Because I've been searching for someone just like you.

A million tears I've cried.
Because I've found many others who aren't you.

A million drops of blood have been shed.
Because I cut out the sorrows I lived with without you.

A million words I've used.
To tell you how much I love you.

A million times I've worn my heart on my sleeve.
Searching for a heart like yours.

A million kisses you've given.

One time.
I will say, "I do".

---

because of you

Because of you this weathered pen,
I no longer write tales of sorrows.
Now I write tales of love so true.

Because of you the crimson blade,
Is laid to rest.
Now it tells tales of yesterday.

Because of you these stitched wounds,
No longer bleed.
Instead help those to learn.

Because of you this blackened soul,
No longer cries.
Now sings songs of happiness.

Because of you this worn body,
No longer confines in shadows.
Instead moves forward shooting for the stars.

Because of you my tired eyes,
No longer show the pain.
Instead warmth and understanding.

Because of you these lines I write,

Showing the world what true love is.
No longer spinning tales of pain and sorrows.

---

caleb was a boy

He bought her a white dress.
Waited at the end of the isle.

She could only see him.
She's been waiting for this for awhile.

He brought her home.
Took her to bed.

She blessed him with a baby girl.
A fruit of life from the life they lead.

He grew old.
One day he passed.

She held her sorrows.
Knowing they wouldn't last.

They met again.
Discovered good–bye didn't mean forever.

rest in peace

Rest in peace my broken heart.
For he has stolen you and fixed you again.

Rest in peace my tearful eyes.
For he has dried your sorrows.

Rest in peace my razor blade.
For he has laid you to rest forevermore.

Rest in peace my darkened soul.
For he gave you light.

Rest in peace my withered vanity.
For he believes no one more beautiful then I.

Rest in peace my burning hate.
For he replaced you with love.

Rest in peace yesterday.
For he has gifted me with today.

teddy bear

Tears start to fall down my face.
The moment I feel that empty space.
I taste your lips.
I see your face.
One moment here.
Nothing to fear.
Next moment gone.
Everything's wrong.
A piece of you to hold dear.
Always keep your heart here.
How can this be?
To be so far away from me?
But hes so close.
The one I love the most.
Memories in my head.
I pour myself into bed.
All this too much to bare
The only one I'm holding tight at night,
My *Teddy bear*.

nick ransom

Nick Ransom is an eclectic, jack-of-all-trades kind of guy. He's a musician, writer, visual artist, cooking fanatic and, oddly enough, avid DIYer.
Writing on topics ranging from the zombie apocalypse, to theological quandries, to good old fashioned revenge, if its on the darker side of things, Nick Ransom would probably take a whack at it in one medium or another.
Inspired heavily by personal experience, dreams, and music, his work ranges from nightmare-inducing stories of vengeance to heartbreak, and absolute loss.

Nick lives in upstate New York, watches too much Star Trek, and spends his time with two wonderful insane people, and two equally wonderful (and equally insane) dogs.

Writing
http://www.fictionpress.com/u/661234/N_Chaos

Visual Art
http://www.atephobic.deviantart.com/

Etsy
http://www.etsy.com/people/nickransom?ref=si_pr

wearing the inside out

rotface

lucid with or without you

michael kohlman

 Life's foisted miseries are not good excuses for missing out on aspects of life that provide enjoyment and reward. I love life's adventure and the ability that I have of figuring life out; until God grabs me by the nape of the neck and tells me to try again. I was almost destroyed when a pursued loved one died, and never having to want to go through that again, I had a lot of thinking and came up with a way to accept life's injustices. I lived that way realizing that the only way to know if I am doing things right is for something to happen again. It did when my mother survived a cardiac arrest at home and suffered severe brain damage. Well, it worked and in this life a good portion of Mike's devotion has been trying to make life better for other people. I strive for success, but that usually relies on other people to foster it as well. I put as much as I can and though success is important, I don't make it a top priority and simply enjoy trying. I am now trying to incorporate my many pursuits into one cohesive product and would love to add the element of performance into the mix. I will do my best, until I drop for the last time!

well, what will it be? trick or treat?

Jonathan Wooten lived in a more sedate Baltimore neighborhood of single houses for some time and while considered a loner, was perceived as the nicest guy in the world; even though much wasn't known about him. He always seemed to be around when the neighbors needed a bit of a hand.

His was a typical story of military service, then worked and with a nice pension he settled down in an early retirement bolstered by a few investments that went his way. Not known to his neighbors was the fact that he enjoyed a brief marriage in another state, which ended early as his wife had terminal cancer and died.

That put the damper on the rest of his life in finding a relationship, but his biggest regret was in not having children with her. His promise to her was he wasn't going to squander himself, but if the right woman came along, she would have to understand and pick him up in heaven as sloppy seconds.

To fill his void with children, he enjoyed every minute with the neighborhood kids that he could afford. Even if totally exhausted and sore, he couldn't resist a game of tag using the edge of his garden as base. Despite his age, he was always in good condition as vowed until his Lord took him away.

While the kids loved him as he was the go between their understanding of how they wanted the world to be, and their parent's demands on them. He helped by being the sublime voice of wisdom talked in a way the kids themselves would understand.

With today's modern word, their parents always kept an eye on him, but he invited it as he never would invite a child into his home without another parent present. A trick he learned from the Boy Scout's youth policy. Those parents were amazed that he kept track of other troubled adults and even sat at a bus stop for school as a little girl was scared that the same vehicle stalked it.

Needless to say, he alerted both the girl's parents and the police and he even explained his concerns to that driver of a vehicle, who decided never to show up again. That was how much he valued any child that would touch his life. The children realized he was special and recognized that about him.

However across the street, there were two girls that loved him for the father that decided not to be in their life, but in growing up they sort of took him for his own and resented him for talking to their mother, who was to remain perpetually single in their little minds.

They resented him for talking to Mom and got quite mouthy. For John it was grating to hear from a block away, the girls yell, "Are you trying to get sex from my mother!" Needless to say the neighbors heard and actually looked at the over the fence liaison, with their mother as a promising sign for the both of them.

The girls thought of it differently, and in close quarters one put on her sweetness and calmly said to him, "I know what to do with Mom rapists like you!" With that she kicked him in the groin, but as much as he wanted to, he didn't roll around on the ground, but remained standing in defiance and managed to walk home despite it ruining his day of getting the lawn cut.

From then on, those two girls declared war on him and while he had the best feelings for their mother and loved the notion of a readymade family, those girls became his royal pain in the ass. At Halloween he gave all the kids the candy he could afford and found that for his efforts a candle wax embossed message, "We really deserve a treat, not your perverted cheap."

Yet there was more scribbling, that entered his mind as saying, "Redrum," but as if it was written in Russian, until he looked at the mirror across the room and discovered it actually spelled, "Murder!" He had a feeling, he knew who did that and it and only took a couple of weeks for the girls of the woman he wanted to know to confirm it!

"Hey Mr. John! For Halloween, we deserve only a full size candy bar! You're a cheap bastard who never deserves love from anybody, even us ... or our Mom!" Right, there was the hook.

Mr. John was aggravated from all the neighbors commenting to him about the condition of his porch, but there was an opportunity to put his plans into progress. The next summer he got an excavator and the neighbors inquired, since his next door one was an engineer, "Why do you need an excavator with a 22ft reach?

He had a bit of fun, but he came up with a rational explanation as a contractor friend of his lent it to him and it saved him a lot of money as opposed to a rental of a termite; a much smaller version to be used to set a new foundation for the porch.

With everybody working, he scooped out a grand hole for his plans and instead of the new fangled fluorescent orange netting; he used a solid wood barrier so no one could see what he was up to. Then came the time to lay the foundation in concrete, and the engineering neighbor of him questioned why he had two cement trucks, he laughed and said, the first one had the wrong mix.

The second concrete trunk driver had his own questions as why the center of the form was boarded over, and he angrily said, "I saw one of these forms go before and kill a man so I think overkill is a great option to prevent this.

The elderly lady across the street saw everything, and questioned his reinforced construction methods, but he calmly blew her off by saying he needed more protection from her prying eyes and enquiring mouth. Other neighbors knew his politics and inclinations and simply figured he was building a bomb shelter for the war that never would come, much like many of the porches that already existed in the neighborhood, created for the fifties nuclear scare.

By the next Halloween, the porch was complete except of the floor, so he put on a solid floor of heavy wood, and under it about two foot of foam insulation. Every kid that came to him got a treat and a hearty, "Enjoy Halloween." But with the neighbor he liked across the street, the woman was stuck at her house to give out the treats and sent her girls on their own.

The girls for all of the other neighbors they were sugar, spice and everything nice; but when they hit Jonathon's house they said, "Well are you going to give us a treat, or give us cheap and get a trick?"

Jonathon smiled and replied, "Last year you got a treat, now it's your turn for a trick!" With that he kicked the lever that sent them to their quieted doom. Needless to say with the girls not returning, their mother was totally upset and reported them missing. While distressing for the mother, she did get a chuckle out of his suggestion for putting signs up for them like lost dogs and cats.

"I understand why you would think that, Johnnie the girls went without and I never had the heart to correct them."

While the police admired Jonathon and knew how much he cared for the children of the community; because he was a loner and single, they had to investigate and were happy that he cooperated and let them search his house. He was cleared of any wrong doing, yet speculation and rumors abounded, but in time that quieted as well.

They say the hero always gets the woman in the end, but in Jonathon's case, his neighbor and the woman he liked was so bereaved, she moved to the city she grew up in and lived forever single in an apartment. While this broke Jonathan's heart, ironically another woman who was single and with children moved into the house she sold.

To all the kids Jonathon Wooten was still that wonderful person as he was to their parents; no one ever forgot the speculation of his role in the girl's disappearance. Jonathon always knew when the children's behavior was changing, as the kids knocked on his door at Halloween and he heard the parents on the sidewalk, laugh and yell, "Don't forget to say, 'Trick or treat!'"

The new neighbor, her children, and Jonathon loved the relationship as he offered the same, and his labors in life were moderated with Frisbee, tag, barbecue and walks on the trails in the park. However, should things once again change; he remembered that Biblical talk that a good relationship is set on a firm foundation.

Even if he has to give up that crazy bomb shelter, and it only end up only the a front porch ... Other parent's always enjoyed his counseling when they had problems with their own kids- "With a little patience, the kids always get it in the end!"

conor carlisle

My name is Conor Carlisle. I'm 17 years old, living in Britain. I started writing poetry when I was 16, doing my GCSE's. I was practicing descriptive pieces for my English exam, and I always put in a few poetic elements in them because I enjoyed analyzing poetry during English classes and I like to be creative. I then decided to start writing poetry in my free time because I found it was a good creative outlet and generally fun to do. It started out pretty basic but I kept going until I started to get better and began to develop my skills more (I'm still trying to improve though). My main influences in writing are Carol-Anne Duffy and Simon Armitage, I read some of their work while doing GCSE English and whenever I'm trying to do a piece that stands out from the rest of my work I try follow the formats of some of their poems. I still enjoy writing and I don't plan to stop, but I never figured that I would actually start writing poetry, especially considering I didn't start talking until I was 3!

http://guy011.deviantart.com

i was in fire at the time

The cackling of crows echo from the church spire
and spikes set upon a school fence bid thee welcome.

I think someone said something about somebody but I can't remember,
I was on fire at the time.

Putting into perspective all that presently persists
our minds in the form of mind games
gives way for comparison of situations and intentions,
when there is nothing else to do
but let the lash of boredom whips
dully open wounds never truly shut.

Some interpretation and representation of deeds and doings
all eventually root to the basic of the king complex.
And emotion is lost within these halls, those one-way corridors,
and distraction among your cell mates
keeps bringing you back to that realization.
Something in the teachings got infected,
a virus of doubt latched onto the jumble of equations.

But home won't make a difference,
you can free me from a place, not a burden.

jewel encrusted eyes

I stand in a penumbra of exclusion,
you on moons edge of class, hand outstretched,
we lie togetherly apart.
I pray for silk sheets
while you beg for burlap bedding.
The class of the upper class lowers
in my presence, in my proximity and those like me,
with standards not of propriety, but decency.
We all know how this tale of tragedy is told...

Icy flames surge in thy peer's eyes
outmatched barely by the fire mark'd
upon thy face and in thy heart.
O such archaic views!
O the irony that the incestuous impose their ideals,
Tis clear! Tis clear! That 'ere is where true propriety lies.
I stand with chainmail rags of mine
and a mop partisan,
aside thee,
who grasps a shield of parchment
as others on this ballroom battlefield
beseech thee to sheath thy quill
of quail and gold.
O such usurpers they be!
Be their minds so narrow
and their judgement worthy of satire
that their jewel encrusted eyes
are blind to the blaring fact
that if my life was "weeded" from yours
that I'd beg for a vibrant blue,

the serene scent of the grave
to flood down my ear or slip down my throat
to save me from my life!

Typical tragedy tells of tears flooding our coffins
but why would this be our story
when bullets have relieved the duty of the rapier
and new lives and new starts are nothing new in this world?
In this age a lean is luxurious
and the modern man may not always be so materialistic
and jewel encrusted eyes can still sometimes see clearly.

popping pods

Little popping pods.
A simple little pinch
and the seeds rocket out, and the skin resends.
We find a field of them, and revoke to a basic fascination.
Slightest touch or tightest grasp,
whether we squeeze the pods or shake the plant,
we find a way to cause them to curl up,
satisfy our search for shock and awe for a split second,
seeing the seed wriggle out reluctantly,
or fly out with full force in a silent explosion,
be it with a delay and disappointment,
dead on with our expectations,
or a random outburst to be met with an outburst of amusement.
White tip, green tip, large and small,
we experiment and observe,
which does what,
to feed a hunger for knowledge and excitement.
We spot little ladybirds, beautiful and bright,
and admire their delicate originality,
as we bash down their habitats to get to those blasting buds.
A wasp stings one of us, a warning that we would be wise to stop.
We laugh it off and continue on.
Even mother joins in, quick to find amazement.
Father frowns of course, but why should I have remorse?
You can't stop me, I'm humanity!
Ah, little popping pods.
Oh, destructive fun.

red spectacles

You would've thought as I did,
that when Jesus started walking waterborne,
he'd have the decency to drag someone back to shore,
help me out a little.

Does grief give us delusions that blind us,
and we merely see the peripheral view,
so we ignore the path, the plan,
that the all-mighty painted before us?
Or is it just
that the faithful, the "reborn",
are actually blind without red spectacles?

Cross me off the list,
life has crowned me too many times.
I drag my weight, bound to this fate,
by faith, as hopeful fantasies are bled out by the sting of reality.
Hoist me up to high heaven,
so I can holler out all holy hell for the above.

Made in his image, that explains a lot.
Why we bleed and are left unhealed,
why lips that sadistically snicker aren't sealed,
the true origin of original sin,
and why the peripheral protagonist will never win.

skin of atmosphere

Sympathy's worth shit.
Give Empathy a shot.
Then the seed will grow
with leaves spurting out your ears.

Give the earth your body
and feel your body take up the earth.
Swap veins for roots, let water run to your heart.
Swap carbon flesh for carbon flesh,
and feel your new blood boil.
Get ice to replace your face (to match the previous heart)
and feel it melt, to expose a flaming skull.
Let the earth have your lungs and breathe the clean air
while you have splinters and shards sticking out your neck
with the occasional saw and digger,
and breathe the heavy dioxide and choke upon it.

Feel the earth suffer inside you,
the salt and sugar strangling it
while you live in blissful content and a habitable environment.
Well, it once was, till you sickened it, in the literal sense.

Sympathy's worth shit.
Give empathy a shot.
See if you don't start choking on dirt.

the masokiss

Give me the Masokiss,
slit my heart and watch it bleed and break,
as my physical being takes pleasure and pleads for more.
Chained in the knowledge that we will never be,
bound and broken and begging for it to be merely the beginning,
as locked lips lash at my love-struck state,

<pre>
                        tango
          tongues   till the peak
      as   of excitement and excruciating pain
    rises   and I plummet and tumble
intensity   nto trustful, tearing tears.
</pre>

The Masokiss is over,
and my lips sigh in satisfaction,
as I am left to bleed
through sensitive, soft synapses
frail and frightened.

The narcissist

He wakes up in the morning, dives off the bunked,
flings off his top and starts changing.
It is then that he catches a glance of a fine figured boy in the mirror.
He leans back in curiosity of this familiar stranger,
questioning the stone structured abs.
In the same second of the curiosity starting it ends,
with a shrug of the shoulders and a turn to the wardrobe.
He opens his cupboard of colors to find the rack of rainbows,
grabbing that which is closest and shoving it on.

He snatches up the comb and rams it through his hair,
ripping out the knots.
He tramples down the stairs dashing into the kitchen.
He kindly greets his mother
as he sends simple smiles to his siblings.
He takes his toast to go as he informs mother
he needs to go into town.
He gets into to town on his own two feet
and navigates through the maze of malls, the circus of civilization.
He passes familiar faces of school friends
and says hi to them subtly and swiftly.
He walks into the park, inhaling the sweet summer scent
as the sunny day blows in the breeze,
with warmth and fresh air soothing his senses.
He lies back upon an oak bench and feels the whole world
turn around that bench, that park, that town,
as he waits for his friends so the great morning
can erupt into a glorious day.

Now we know how he views the world,
so now let's see how the world views him.

He wakes up in the morning and jumps down
from his excessive and needless bunked.
He tears off the top, leans back and tenses
to turn the faint lines on his stomach into oddly shaped abs,
which his mind claims to be marble masterpiece.
An age later he opens up the wardrobe
packed with designer clothes not worn half the time.
Mother starts making a full fry up
the moment he opens the wardrobe,
and finishes and serves it
the moment he's decided what he wants to wear.

He grabs the comb and gently runs it
through his perfectly conditioned hair.
When the family is almost full, he gets his parting just right.
He then storms down the staircase,
knocking plants and photos with no remorse.
He enters the kitchen, with a subtle demand for attention.
He bumps brothers and shoves sisters, smirking at them
and matching their sorrowed looks with mocking grins.
He snatches the toast from their plates
and whilst scoffing their breakfast he brutishly bellows
"I'm going out!" to his mother, his maid.
He enters the citadel, the great outdoor halls,
the playground of his little world.
He passes the schoolgirls of his class,
who scoff and scowl at his gross gestures and sly smiles.
He struts through the pleasant park,
his attitude infecting the atmosphere.
A family tries to take rest from a strenuous stroll
but finds the last bench hogged, by a stubborn snob.
He waits like a panther to pounce upon those
he believes are his friends,
who made plans and falsely assumed it was in private from him.
He is happily unaware that those he plots to leech upon
have seen him and fled, like an incoming blitz terrorizing the
streets.
He remains blissfully ignorant from the fact
that the population of the park
judges that spoilt slime, lying on the bench,
trapped in the delusion that the whole world
revolves round him, his twisted thoughts, his selfish mind, his black
heart.

www.ingramcontent.com/pod-product-compliance
Lightning Source LLC
Chambersburg PA
CBHW040823050726
47507CB00021B/110